DC SUPER HERO GIRLS

™

SUMMER OLYMPUS

an original graphic novel

WRITTEN BY
Shea Fontana

ART BY
Yancey Labat

COLORS BY
Monica Kubina

LETTERING BY
Janice Chiang

MARIE JAVINS Group Editor
BRITTANY HOLZHERR Associate Editor
STEVE COOK Design Director - Books
AMIE BROCKWAY-METCALF Publication Design

BOB HARRAS Senior VP - Editor-in-Chief, DC Comics

DIANE NELSON President
DAN DiDIO Publisher
JIM LEE Publisher
GEOFF JOHNS President & Chief Creative Officer
AMIT DESAI Executive VP - Business & Marketing Strategy,
Direct to Consumer & Global Franchise Management
SAM ADES Senior VP - Direct to Consumer
BOBBIE CHASE VP - Talent Development
MARK CHIARELLO Senior VP - Art, Design & Collected Editions
JOHN CUNNINGHAM Senior VP - Sales & Trade Marketing
ANNE DEPIES Senior VP - Business Strategy, Finance & Administration
DON FALLETTI VP - Manufacturing Operations
LAWRENCE GANEM VP - Editorial Administration & Talent Relations
ALISON GILL Senior VP - Manufacturing & Operations
HANK KANALZ Senior VP - Editorial Strategy & Administration
JAY KOGAN VP - Legal Affairs
THOMAS LOFTUS VP - Business Affairs
JACK MAHAN VP - Business Affairs
NICK J. NAPOLITANO VP - Manufacturing Administration
EDDIE SCANNELL VP - Consumer Marketing
COURTNEY SIMMONS Senior VP - Publicity & Communications
JIM (SKI) SOKOLOWSKI VP - Comic Book Specialty Sales & Trade Marketing
NANCY SPEARS VP - Mass, Book, Digital Sales & Trade Marketing

PEFC Certified
Printed on paper from
sustainably managed
forests and controlled
sources
www.pefc.org
PEFC/01-31-106

TABLE OF CONTENTS

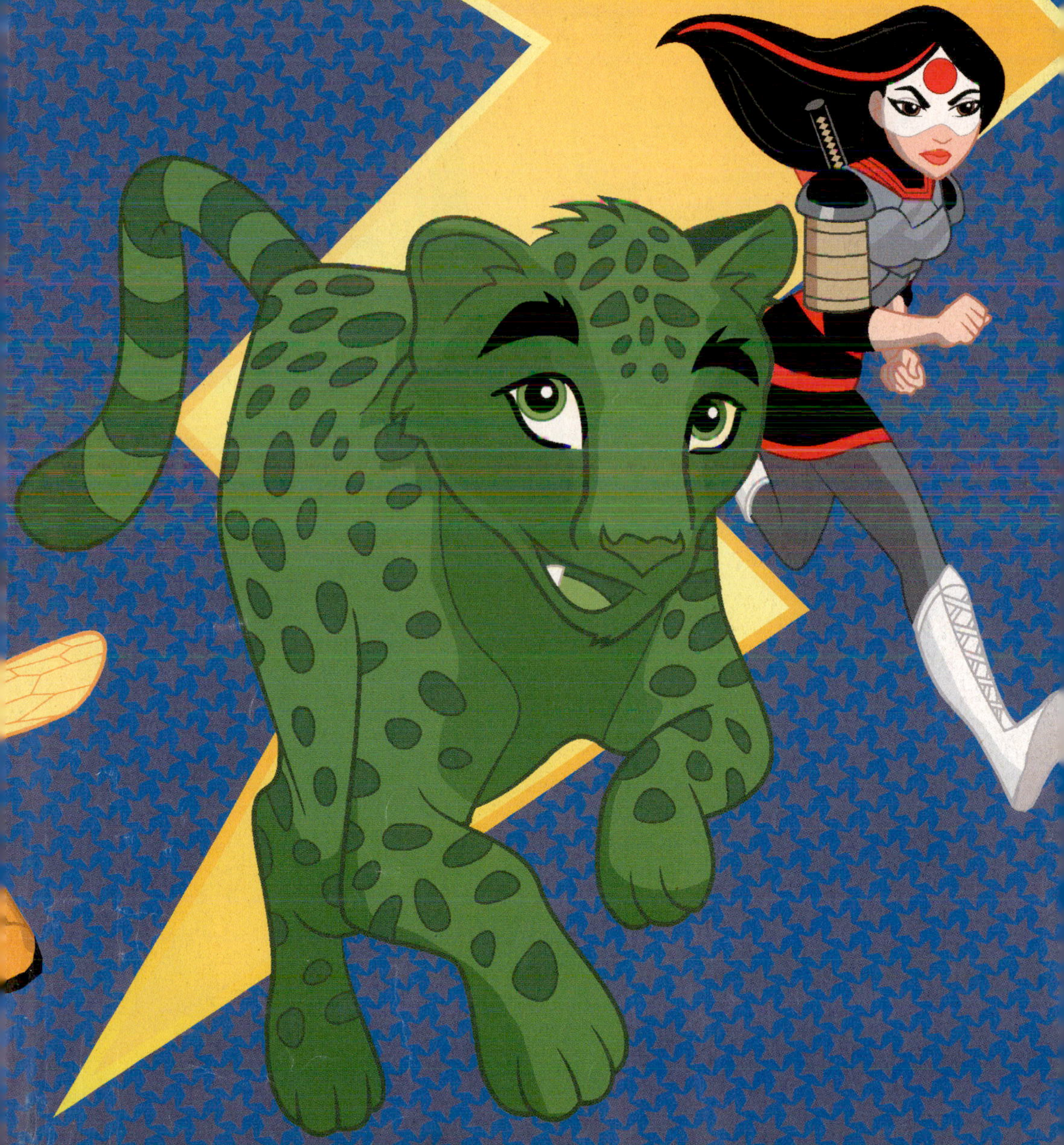

ROLL AT SUPER

SUPER HERO HIGH SCHOOL

WONDER WOMAN

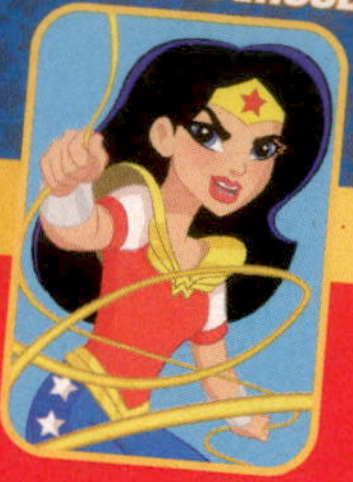

SUPERPOWERS
Super-strength, flight, near-invincibility, super-athleticism

SUPER HERO HIGH SCHOOL

BATGIRL

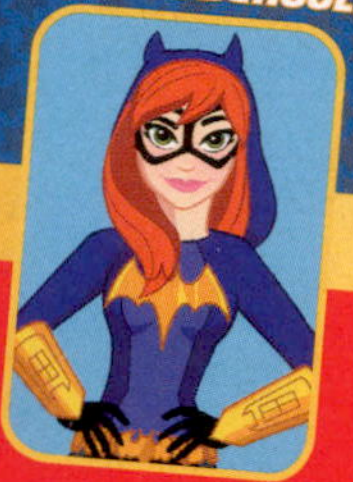

SUPERPOWERS
Computer genius, expert martial artist, photographic memory, legendary detective skills

SUPER HERO HIGH SCHOOL

POISON IVY

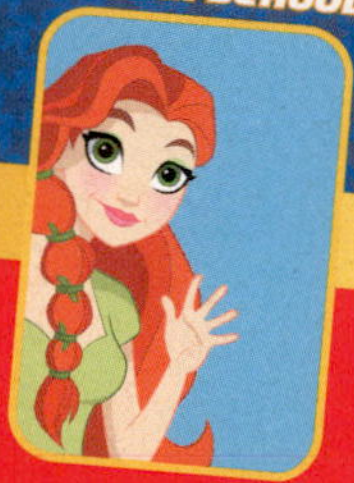

SUPERPOWERS
Genius-level intellect, summons and controls plants

SUPER HERO HIGH SCHOOL

KATANA

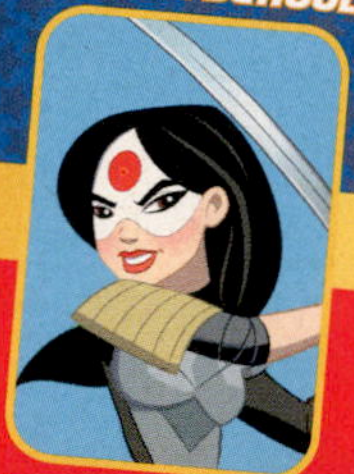

SUPERPOWERS
Superior sword-fighter, expert martial artist, advanced stealth skills

SUPER HERO HIGH SCHOOL

CHEETAH

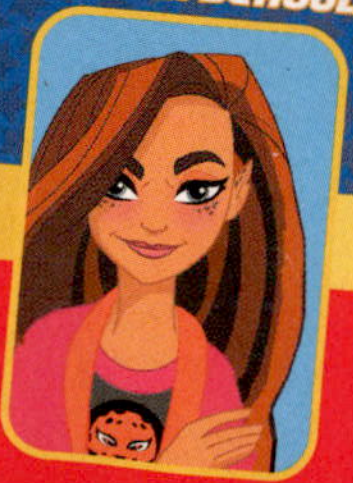

SUPERPOWERS
Agility, speed, sharp reflexes, even sharper claws

SUPER HERO HIGH SCHOOL

SUPERGIRL

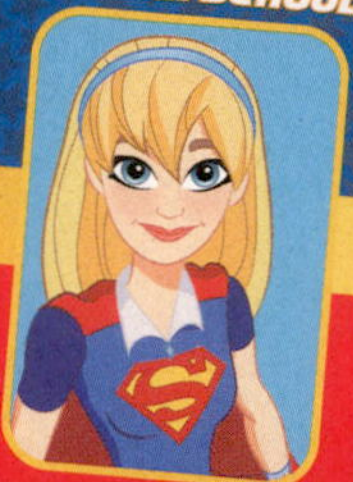

SUPERPOWERS
Super-strength, flight, invincibility, super-hearing, heat vision, x-ray vision

SUPER HERO HIGH SCHOOL

BUMBLEBEE

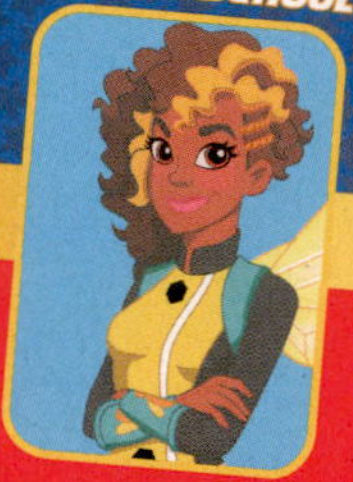

SUPERPOWERS
Enhanced strength, flight, ability to shrink, projects stinger blasts

SUPER HERO HIGH SCHOOL

HARLEY QUINN

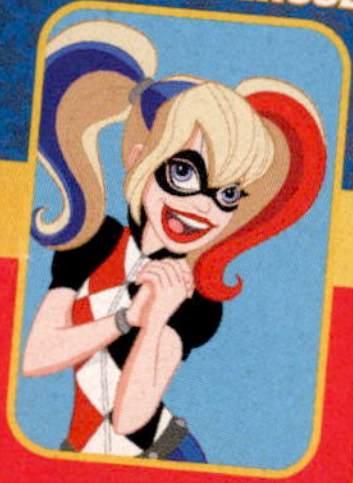

SUPERPOWERS
Expert gymnast, acrobat, quick-witted class clown

SUPER HERO HIGH SCHOOL

BEAST BOY

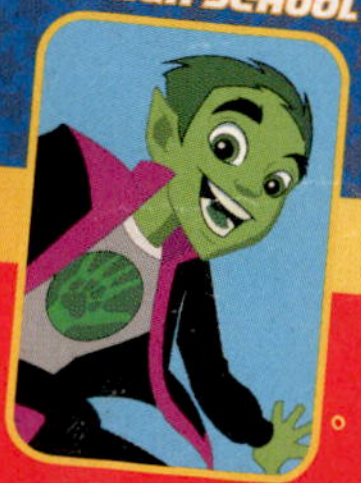

SUPERPOWERS
Shape-shifts into any animal form, world-class slacker

CALL HERO HIGH

SUPER HERO HIGH SCHOOL

SHHS

LADY SHIVA

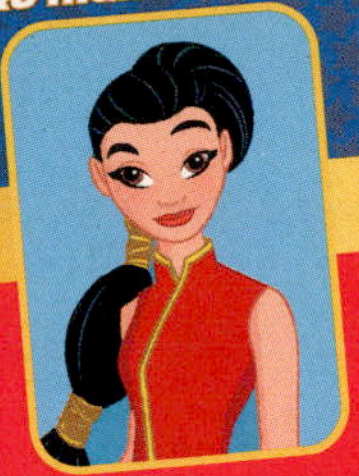

SUPERPOWERS

Expert martial artist, healer, strong-willed, never gives up

SUPER HERO HIGH SCHOOL

SHHS

FLASH

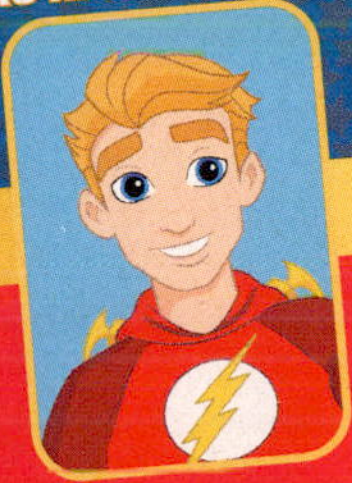

SUPERPOWERS

Super-speed, vibrates his molecules through walls, detective skills

SUPER HERO HIGH SCHOOL

SHHS

HAWKGIRL

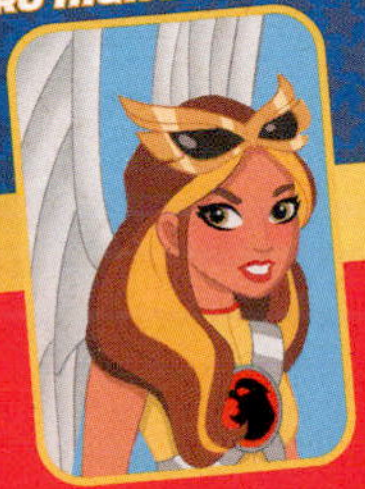

SUPERPOWERS

Flight, super detective skills, weapons expert

SUPER HERO HIGH SCHOOL

SHHS

CATWOMAN

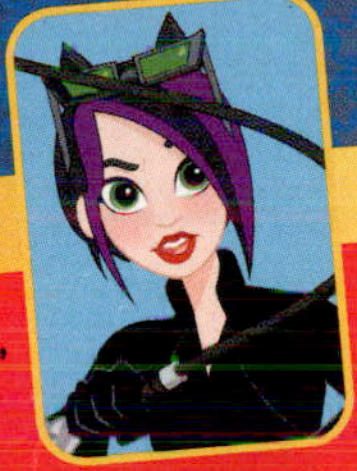

SUPERPOWERS

Super-stealth, master gymnast, acrobat, always lands on her feet, loves cats

SUPER HERO HIGH SCHOOL

SHHS

STARFIRE

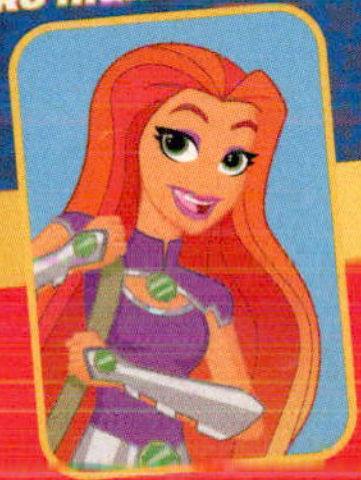

SUPERPOWERS

Flight, super-strength, can shoot star bolts from her hands

SUPER HERO HIGH SCHOOL

SHHS

BIG BARDA

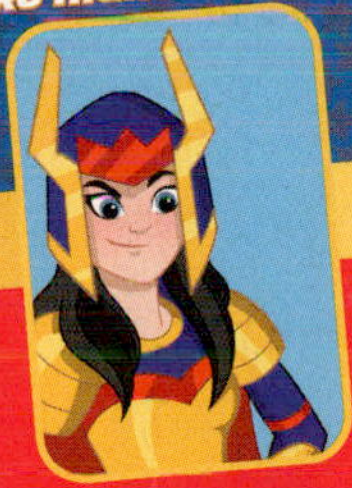

SUPERPOWERS

Invincibility, super-reflexes, super-strength, expert at hand-to-hand combat

SUPER HERO HIGH SCHOOL

SHHS

FROST

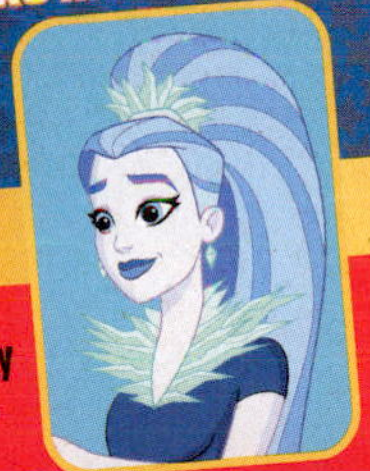

SUPERPOWERS

Scientific genius, absorbs energy and converts it into sub-zero-temperature ice blasts

SUPER HERO HIGH SCHOOL

SHHS

AMANDA WALLER

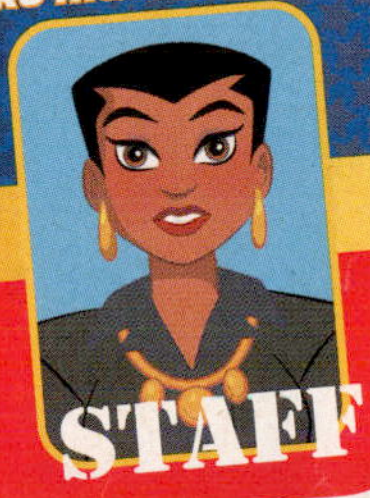
STAFF

Principal, mentor, stern but fair

SUPER HERO HIGH SCHOOL

SHHS

GORILLA GRODD

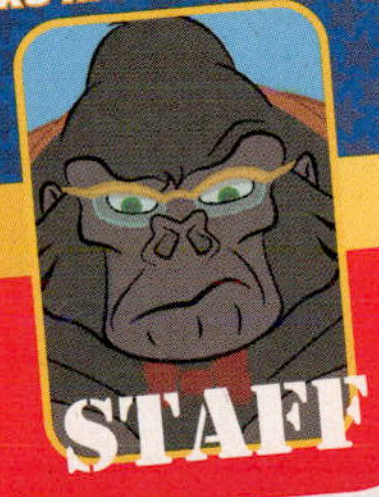
STAFF

Vice Principal, mind-control powers, in charge of detention

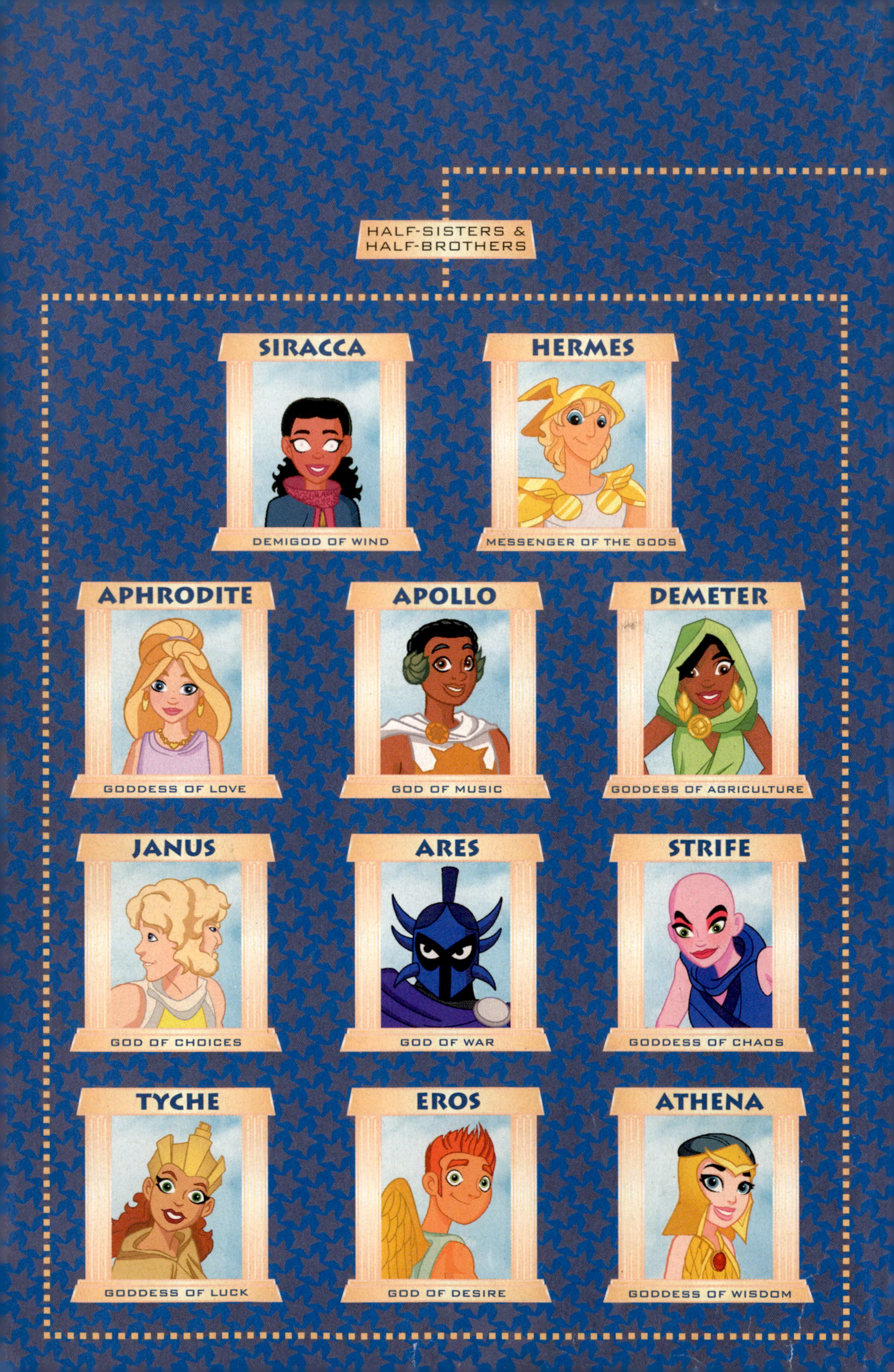
HALF-SISTERS & HALF-BROTHERS
SIRACCA
DEMIGOD OF WIND
HERMES
MESSENGER OF THE GODS
APHRODITE
GODDESS OF LOVE
APOLLO
GOD OF MUSIC
DEMETER
GODDESS OF AGRICULTURE
JANUS
GOD OF CHOICES
ARES
GOD OF WAR
STRIFE
GODDESS OF CHAOS
TYCHE
GODDESS OF LUCK
EROS
GOD OF DESIRE
ATHENA
GODDESS OF WISDOM

WONDER WOMAN'S FAMILY TREE

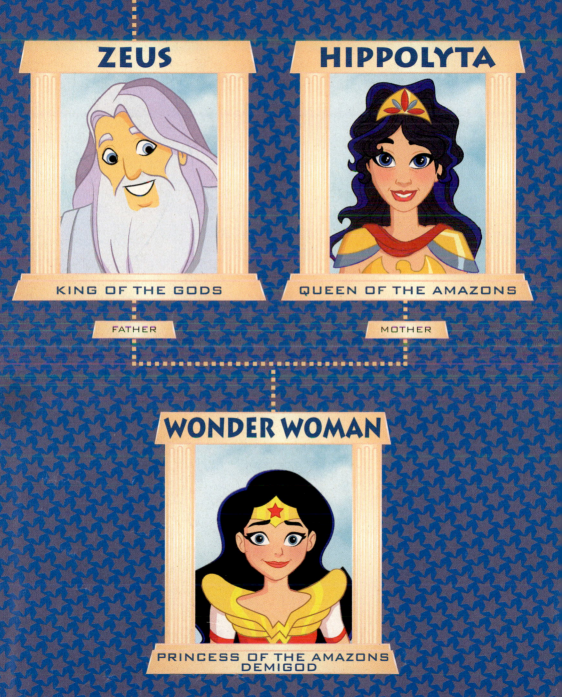

ZEUS
KING OF THE GODS

FATHER

HIPPOLYTA
QUEEN OF THE AMAZONS

MOTHER

WONDER WOMAN
PRINCESS OF THE AMAZONS
DEMIGOD

CHAPTER ONE
GIMME A SUMMER BREAK

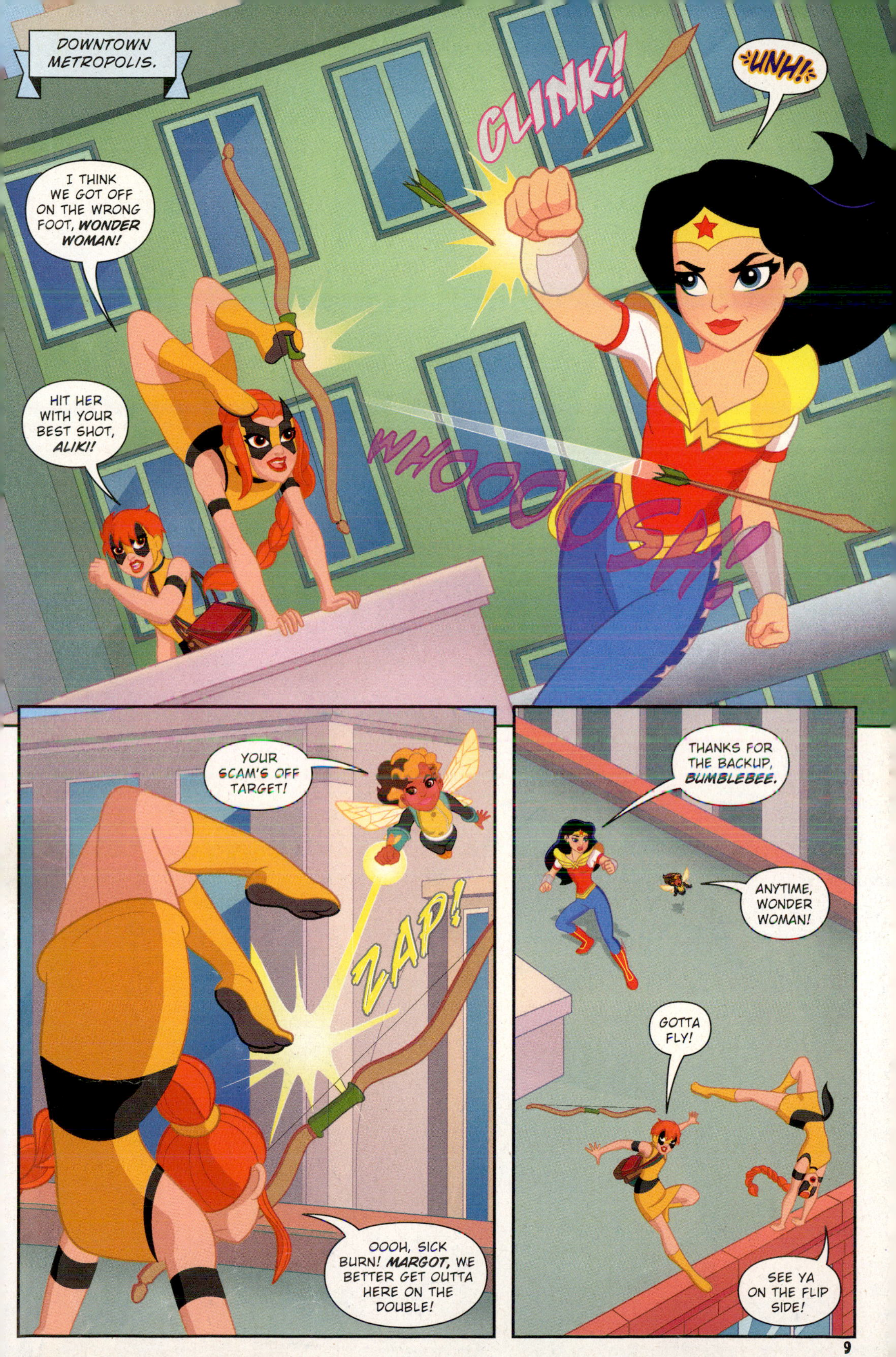
DOWNTOWN METROPOLIS.
CLINK!
UNH!
I THINK WE GOT OFF ON THE WRONG FOOT, WONDER WOMAN!
HIT HER WITH YOUR BEST SHOT, ALIKI!
WHOOOOOSH!
YOUR SCAM'S OFF TARGET!
ZAP!
OOOH, SICK BURN! MARGOT, WE BETTER GET OUTTA HERE ON THE DOUBLE!
THANKS FOR THE BACKUP, BUMBLEBEE.
ANYTIME, WONDER WOMAN!
GOTTA FLY!
SEE YA ON THE FLIP SIDE!

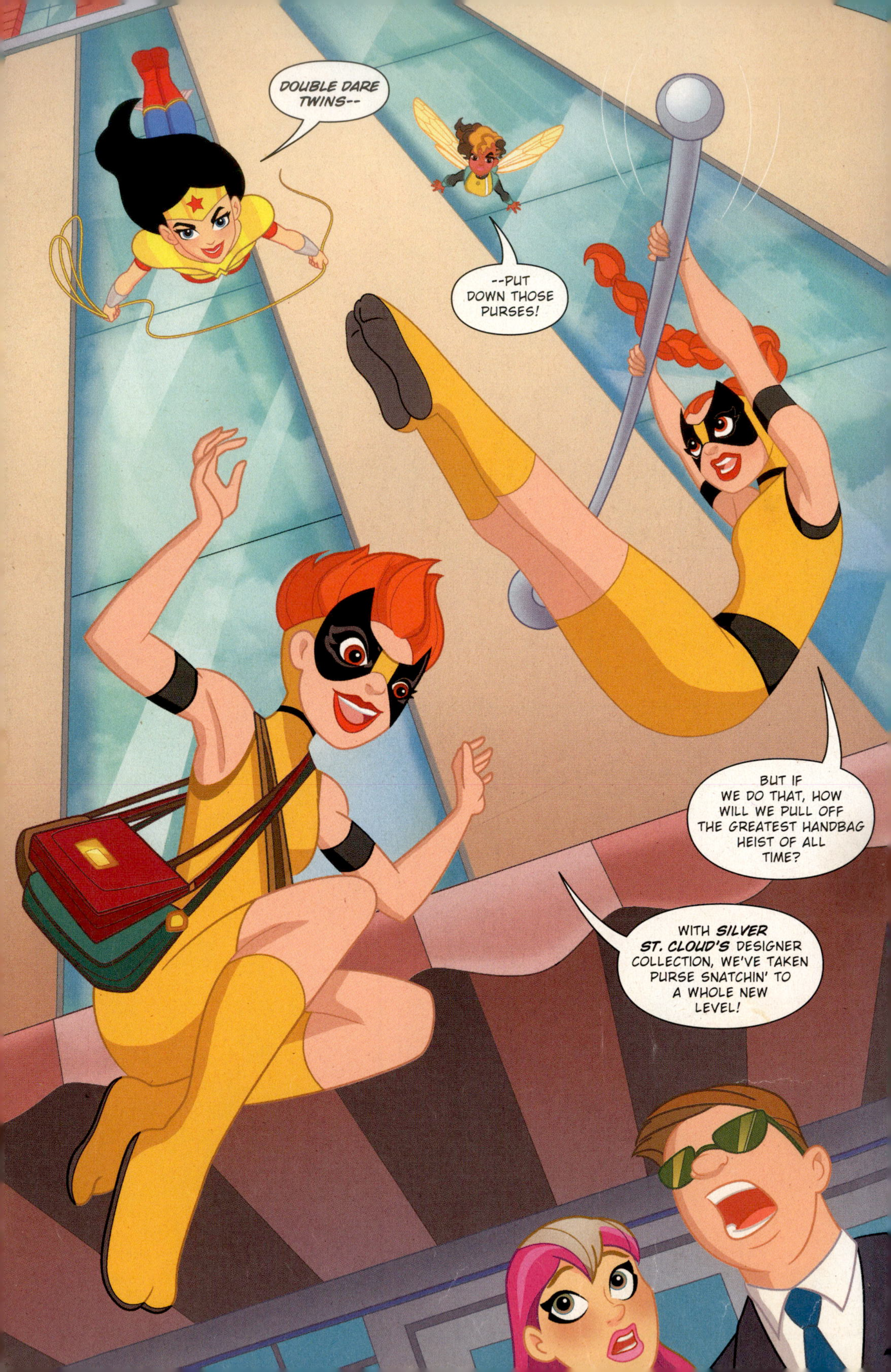
DOUBLE DARE TWINS--
--PUT DOWN THOSE PURSES!
BUT IF WE DO THAT, HOW WILL WE PULL OFF THE GREATEST HANDBAG HEIST OF ALL TIME?
WITH SILVER ST. CLOUD'S DESIGNER COLLECTION, WE'VE TAKEN PURSE SNATCHIN' TO A WHOLE NEW LEVEL!

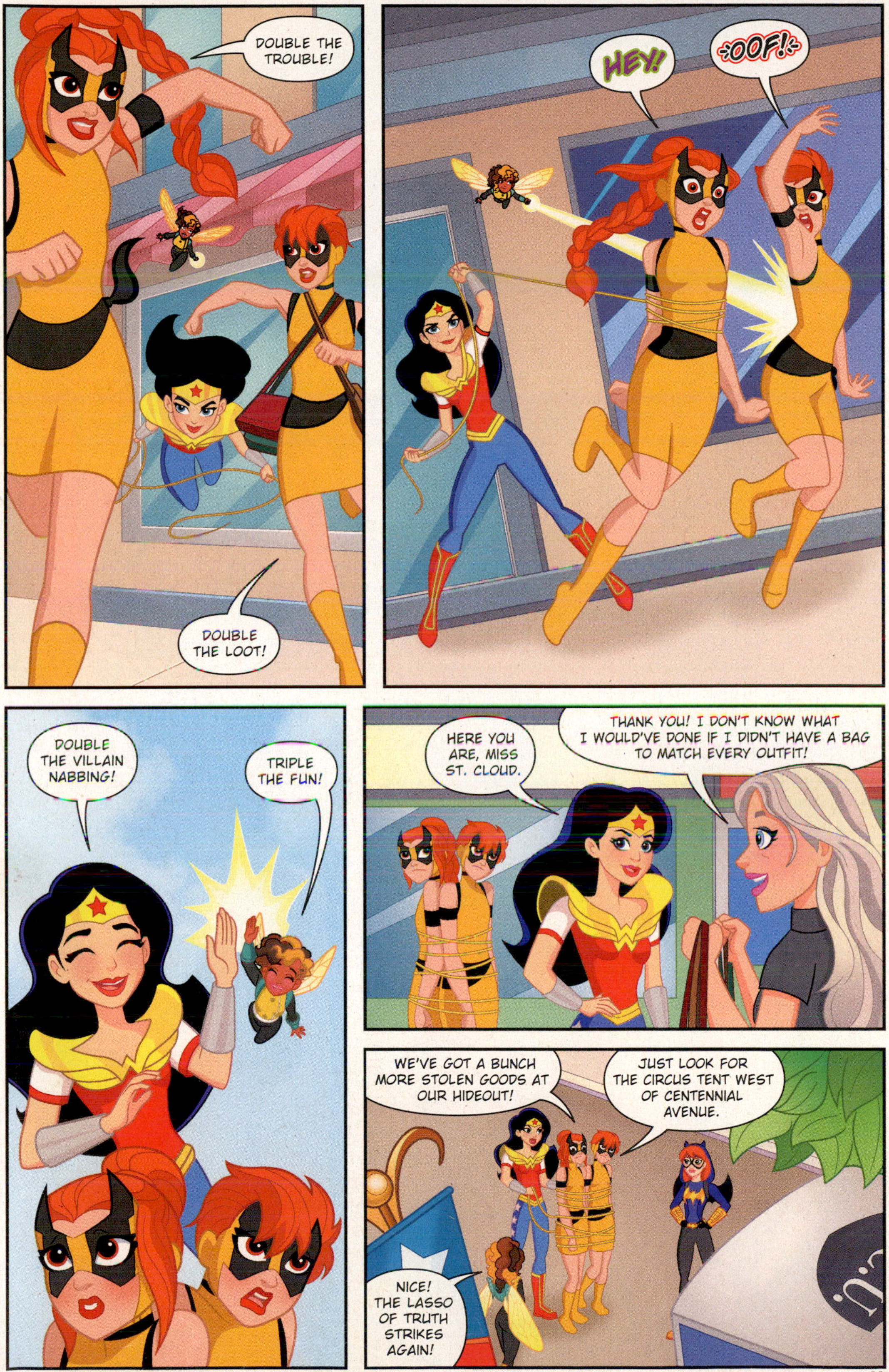
DOUBLE THE TROUBLE!
DOUBLE THE LOOT!
HEY!
OOF!
DOUBLE THE VILLAIN NABBING!
TRIPLE THE FUN!
HERE YOU ARE, MISS ST. CLOUD.
THANK YOU! I DON'T KNOW WHAT I WOULD'VE DONE IF I DIDN'T HAVE A BAG TO MATCH EVERY OUTFIT!
WE'VE GOT A BUNCH MORE STOLEN GOODS AT OUR HIDEOUT!
JUST LOOK FOR THE CIRCUS TENT WEST OF CENTENNIAL AVENUE.
NICE! THE LASSO OF TRUTH STRIKES AGAIN!

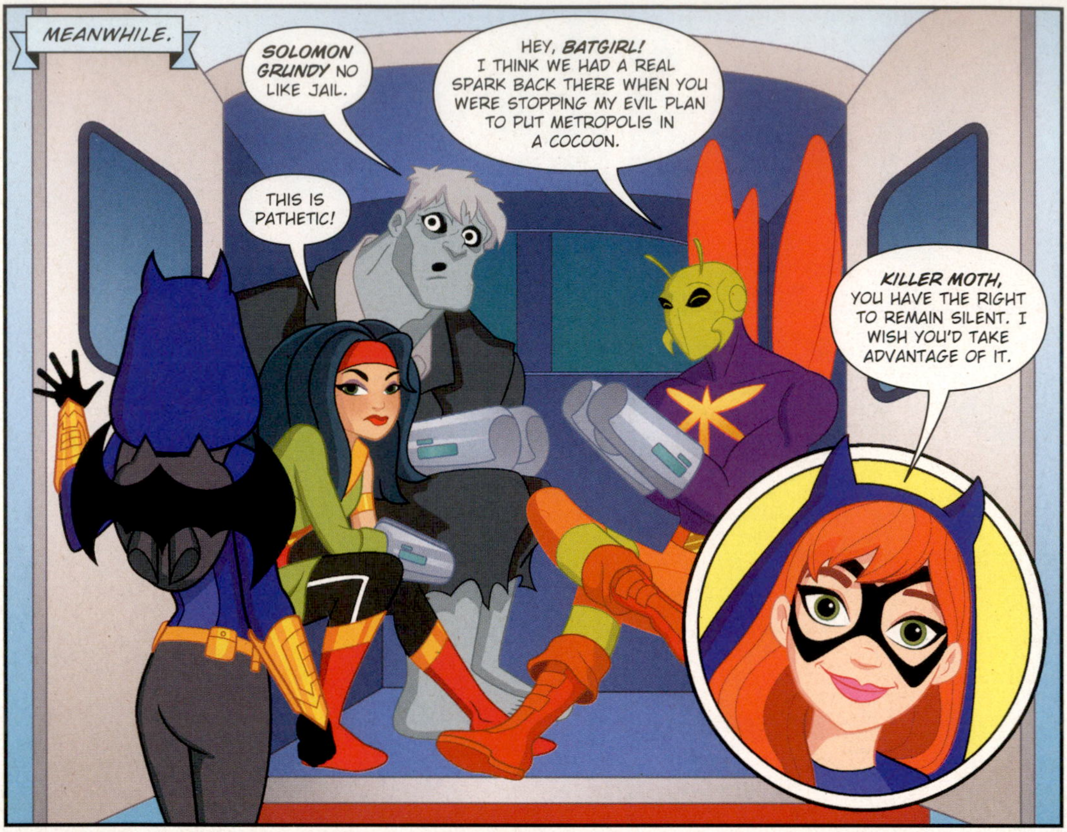
MEANWHILE.
SOLOMON GRUNDY NO LIKE JAIL.
HEY, BATGIRL! I THINK WE HAD A REAL SPARK BACK THERE WHEN YOU WERE STOPPING MY EVIL PLAN TO PUT METROPOLIS IN A COCOON.
THIS IS PATHETIC!
KILLER MOTH, YOU HAVE THE RIGHT TO REMAIN SILENT. I WISH YOU'D TAKE ADVANTAGE OF IT.

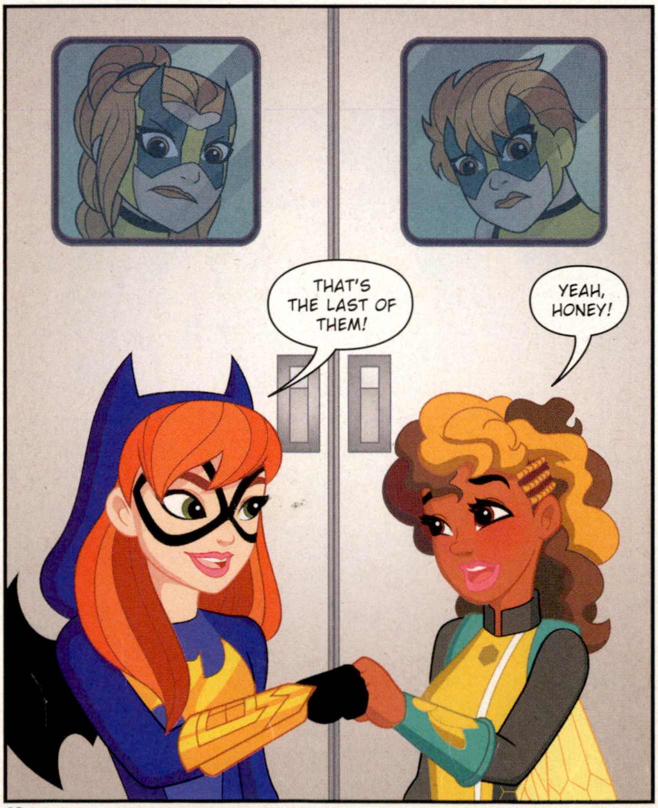
THAT'S THE LAST OF THEM!
YEAH, HONEY!

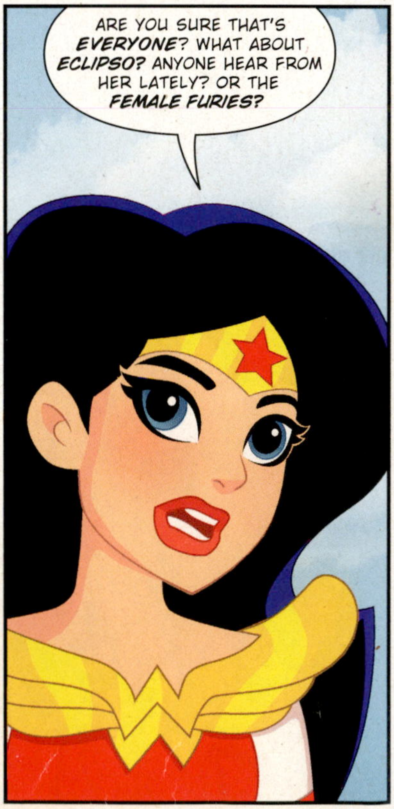
ARE YOU SURE THAT'S EVERYONE? WHAT ABOUT ECLIPSO? ANYONE HEAR FROM HER LATELY? OR THE FEMALE FURIES?

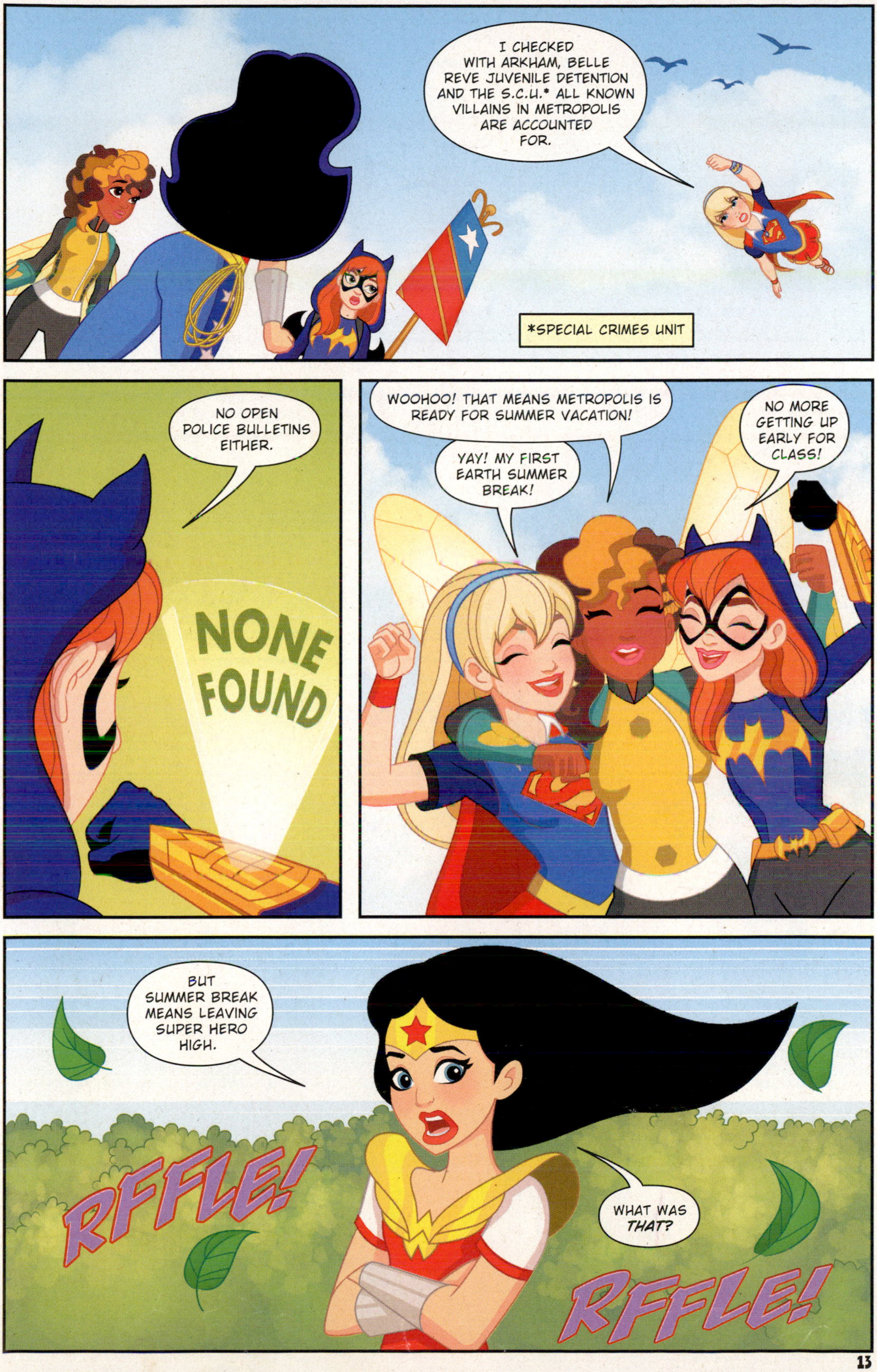
I CHECKED WITH ARKHAM, BELLE REVE JUVENILE DETENTION AND THE S.C.U.* ALL KNOWN VILLAINS IN METROPOLIS ARE ACCOUNTED FOR.
*SPECIAL CRIMES UNIT
NO OPEN POLICE BULLETINS EITHER.
NONE FOUND
WOOHOO! THAT MEANS METROPOLIS IS READY FOR SUMMER VACATION!
YAY! MY FIRST EARTH SUMMER BREAK!
NO MORE GETTING UP EARLY FOR CLASS!
BUT SUMMER BREAK MEANS LEAVING SUPER HERO HIGH.
RFFLE!
WHAT WAS THAT?
RFFLE!

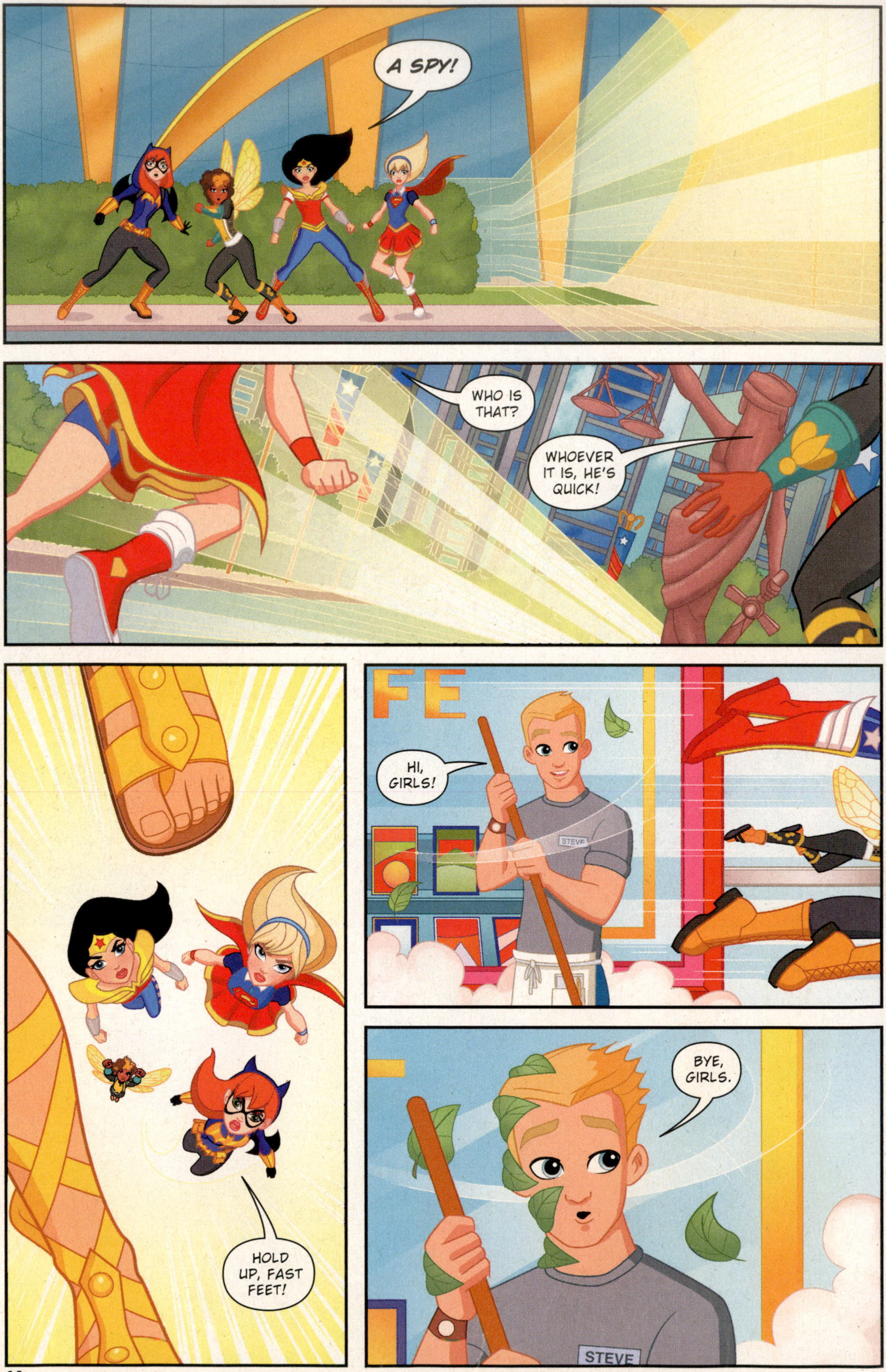
A SPY!
WHO IS THAT?
WHOEVER IT IS, HE'S QUICK!
HOLD UP, FAST FEET!
HI, GIRLS!
STEVE
BYE, GIRLS.
STEVE

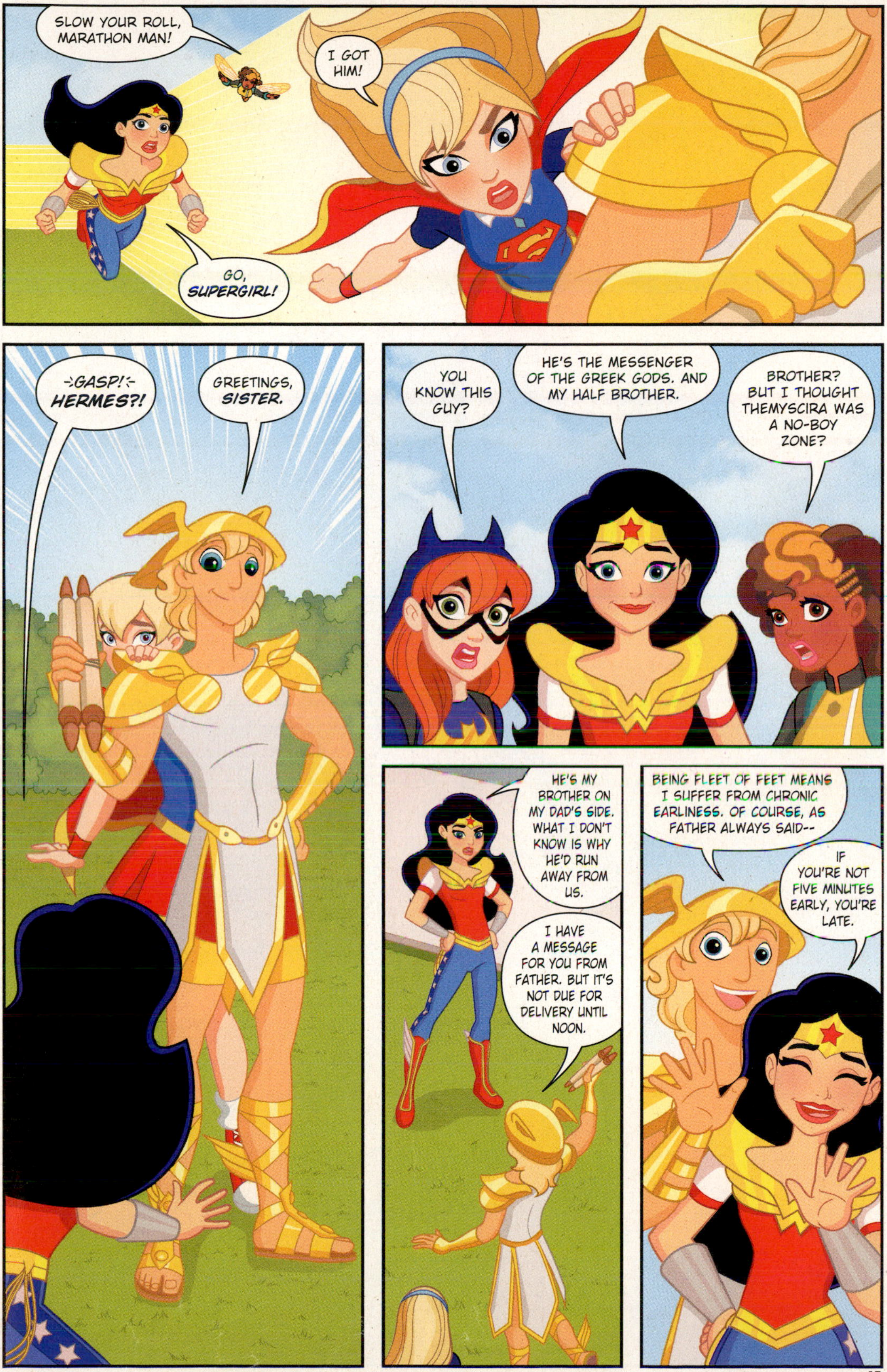
SLOW YOUR ROLL, MARATHON MAN!
I GOT HIM!
GO, SUPERGIRL!
-GASP!- HERMES?!
GREETINGS, SISTER.
YOU KNOW THIS GUY?
HE'S THE MESSENGER OF THE GREEK GODS. AND MY HALF BROTHER.
BROTHER? BUT I THOUGHT THEMYSCIRA WAS A NO-BOY ZONE?
HE'S MY BROTHER ON MY DAD'S SIDE. WHAT I DON'T KNOW IS WHY HE'D RUN AWAY FROM US.
I HAVE A MESSAGE FOR YOU FROM FATHER. BUT IT'S NOT DUE FOR DELIVERY UNTIL NOON.
BEING FLEET OF FEET MEANS I SUFFER FROM CHRONIC EARLINESS. OF COURSE, AS FATHER ALWAYS SAID--
IF YOU'RE NOT FIVE MINUTES EARLY, YOU'RE LATE.

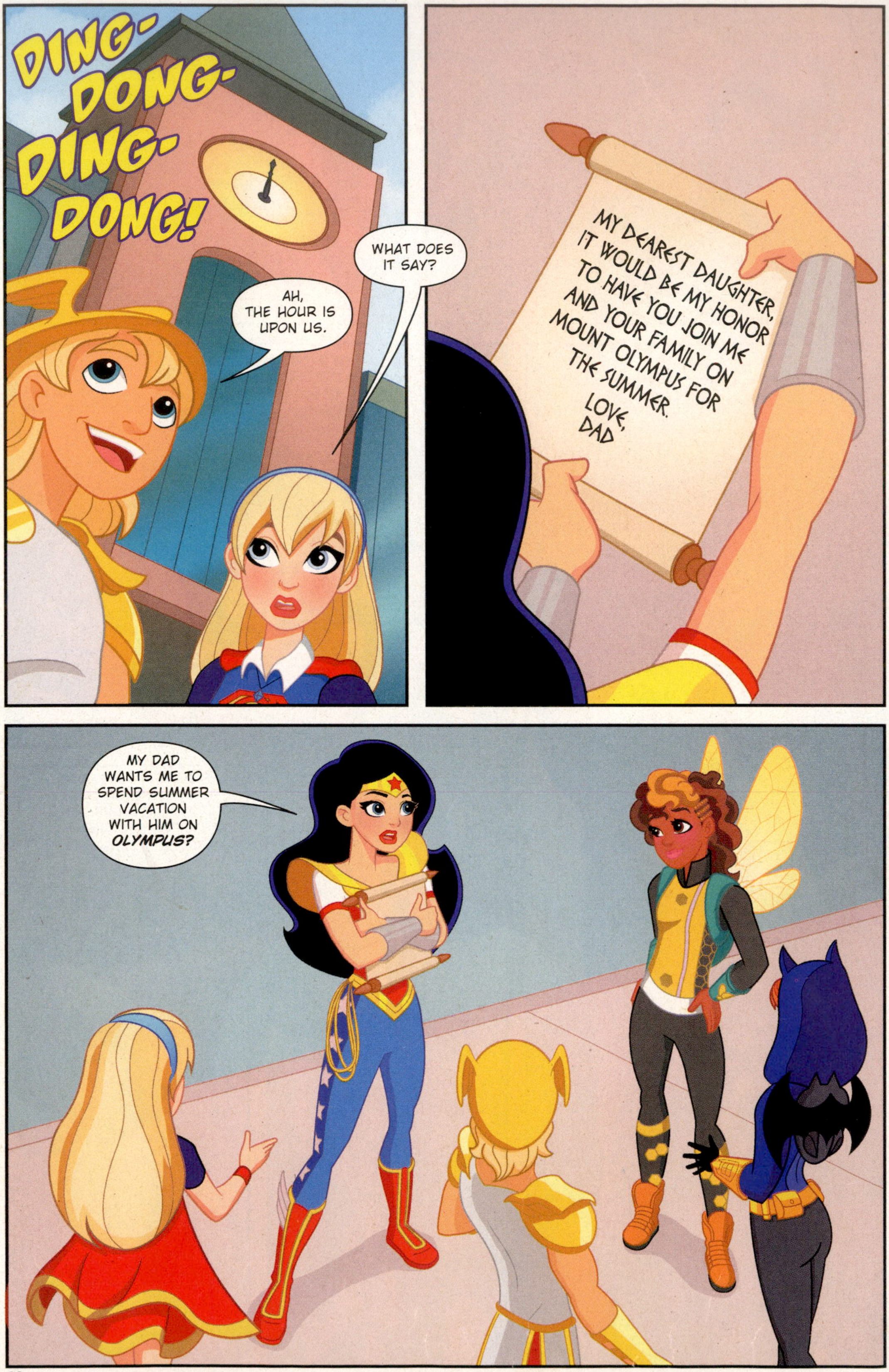
DING-DONG-DING-DONG!
AH, THE HOUR IS UPON US.
WHAT DOES IT SAY?
MY DEAREST DAUGHTER, IT WOULD BE MY HONOR TO HAVE YOU JOIN ME AND YOUR FAMILY ON MOUNT OLYMPUS FOR THE SUMMER. LOVE, DAD
MY DAD WANTS ME TO SPEND SUMMER VACATION WITH HIM ON *OLYMPUS?*

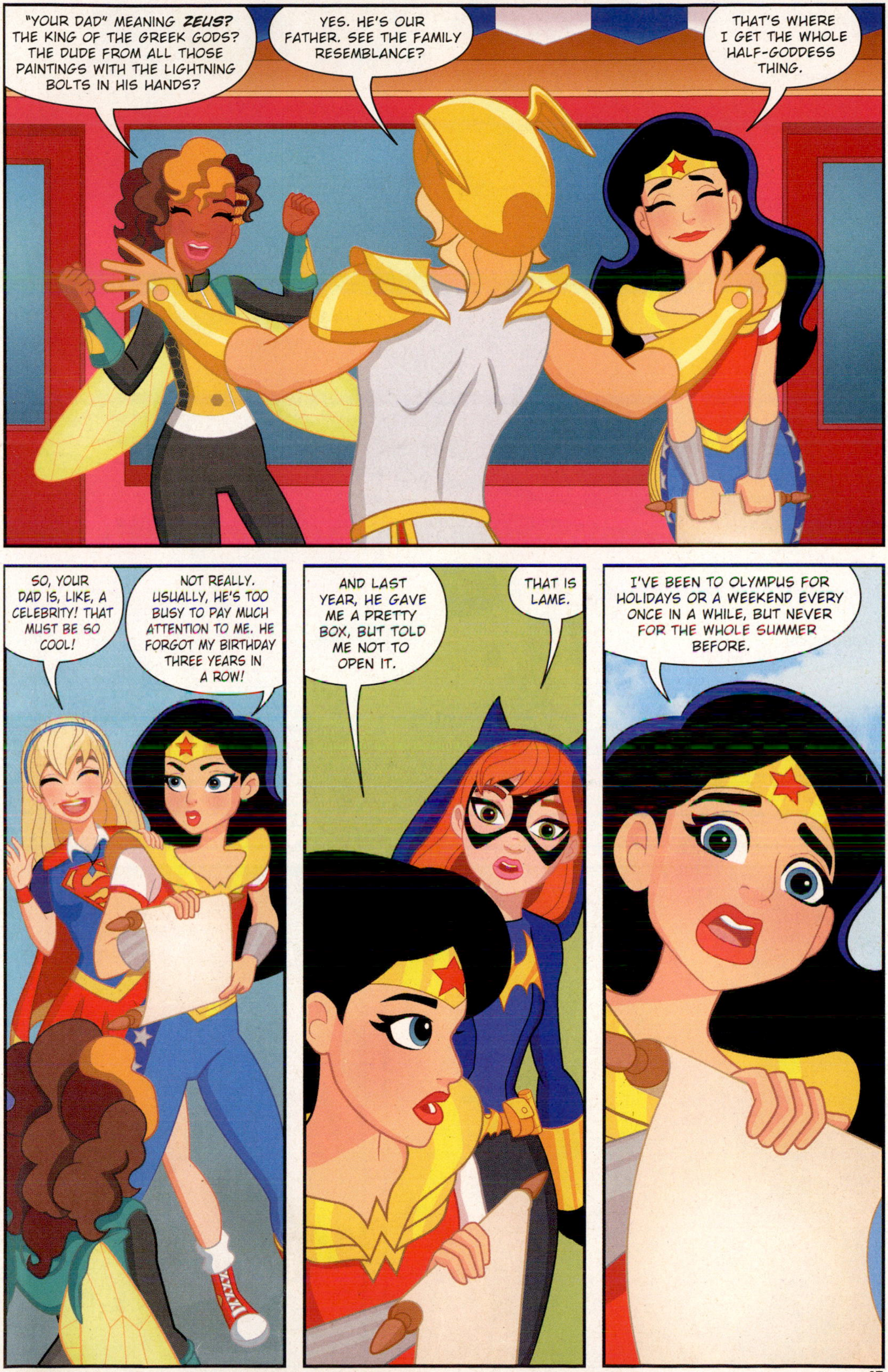
"YOUR DAD" MEANING *ZEUS?* THE KING OF THE GREEK GODS? THE DUDE FROM ALL THOSE PAINTINGS WITH THE LIGHTNING BOLTS IN HIS HANDS?
YES. HE'S OUR FATHER. SEE THE FAMILY RESEMBLANCE?
THAT'S WHERE I GET THE WHOLE HALF-GODDESS THING.
SO, YOUR DAD IS, LIKE, A CELEBRITY! THAT MUST BE SO COOL!
NOT REALLY. USUALLY, HE'S TOO BUSY TO PAY MUCH ATTENTION TO ME. HE FORGOT MY BIRTHDAY THREE YEARS IN A ROW!
AND LAST YEAR, HE GAVE ME A PRETTY BOX, BUT TOLD ME NOT TO OPEN IT.
THAT IS LAME.
I'VE BEEN TO OLYMPUS FOR HOLIDAYS OR A WEEKEND EVERY ONCE IN A WHILE, BUT NEVER FOR THE WHOLE SUMMER BEFORE.

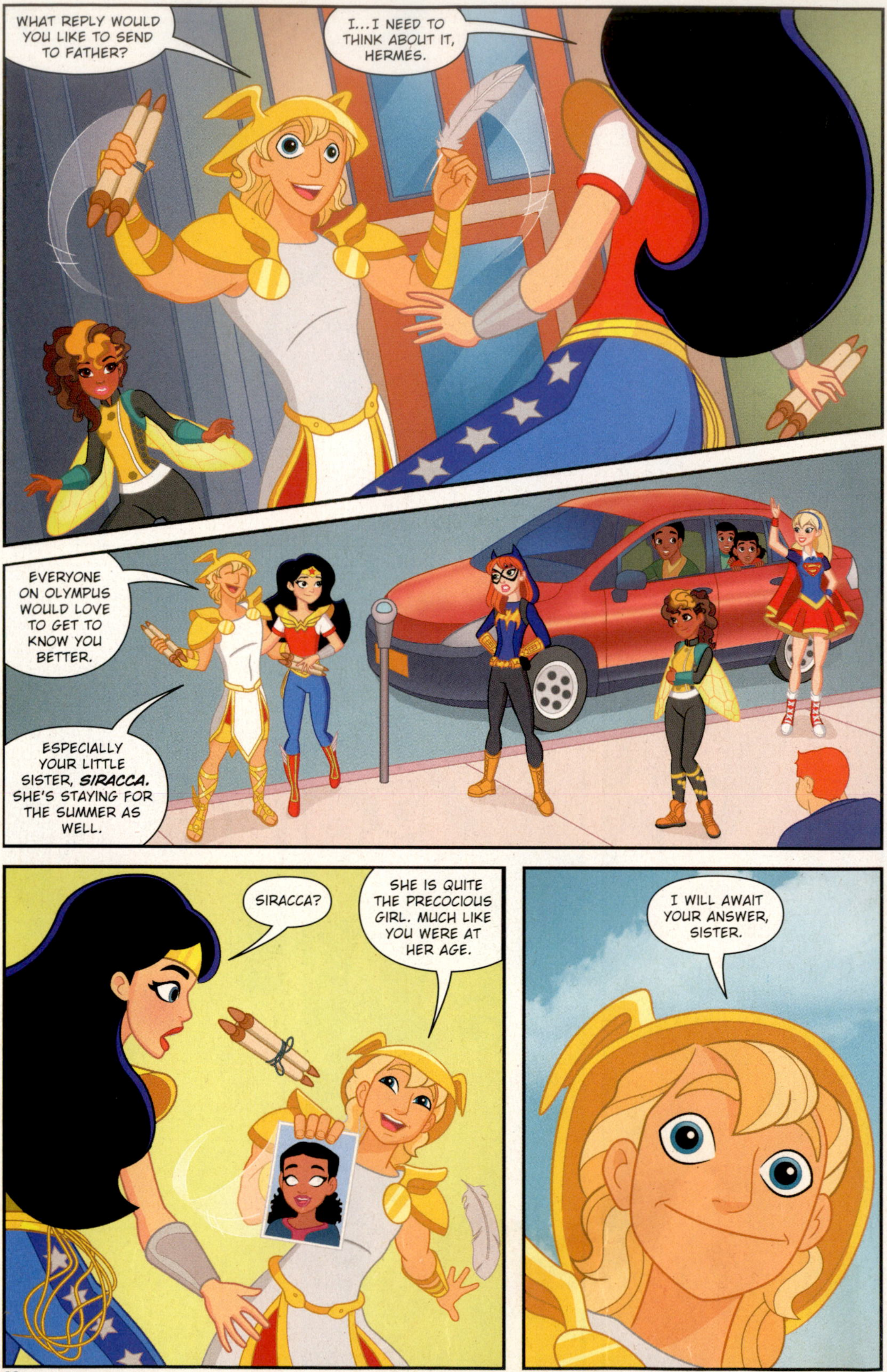
WHAT REPLY WOULD YOU LIKE TO SEND TO FATHER?
I...I NEED TO THINK ABOUT IT, HERMES.
EVERYONE ON OLYMPUS WOULD LOVE TO GET TO KNOW YOU BETTER.
ESPECIALLY YOUR LITTLE SISTER, SIRACCA. SHE'S STAYING FOR THE SUMMER AS WELL.
SIRACCA?
SHE IS QUITE THE PRECOCIOUS GIRL. MUCH LIKE YOU WERE AT HER AGE.
I WILL AWAIT YOUR ANSWER, SISTER.

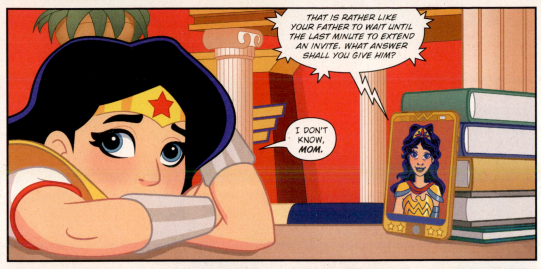

THAT IS RATHER LIKE YOUR FATHER TO WAIT UNTIL THE LAST MINUTE TO EXTEND AN INVITE. WHAT ANSWER SHALL YOU GIVE HIM?

I DON'T KNOW, MOM.

YOU KNOW I LOVE MY AMAZON SIDE AND THEMYSCIRA WILL ALWAYS BE MY HOME.

BUT I HAVE BEEN CURIOUS ABOUT THE GODDESS SIDE OF ME.

BUT OLYMPUS IS SO FAR AWAY. AND FOR THE WHOLE SUMMER? I'LL MISS MY FRIENDS.

KNOCK! KNOCK!

HUH?

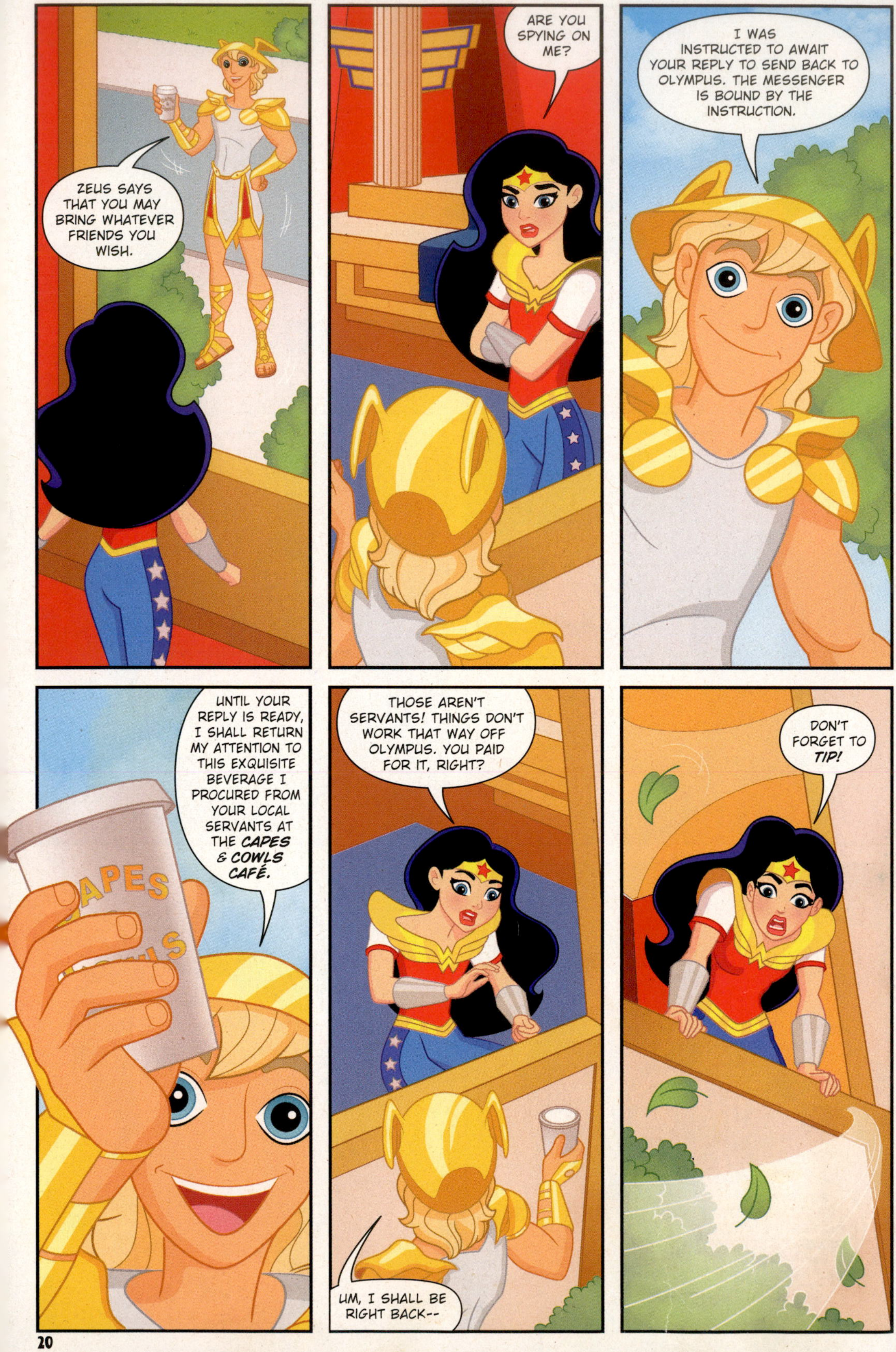
ZEUS SAYS THAT YOU MAY BRING WHATEVER FRIENDS YOU WISH.
ARE YOU SPYING ON ME?
I WAS INSTRUCTED TO AWAIT YOUR REPLY TO SEND BACK TO OLYMPUS. THE MESSENGER IS BOUND BY THE INSTRUCTION.
UNTIL YOUR REPLY IS READY, I SHALL RETURN MY ATTENTION TO THIS EXQUISITE BEVERAGE I PROCURED FROM YOUR LOCAL SERVANTS AT THE *CAPES & COWLS CAFÉ.*
CAPES
THOSE AREN'T SERVANTS! THINGS DON'T WORK THAT WAY OFF OLYMPUS. YOU PAID FOR IT, RIGHT?
UM, I SHALL BE RIGHT BACK--
DON'T FORGET TO *TIP!*

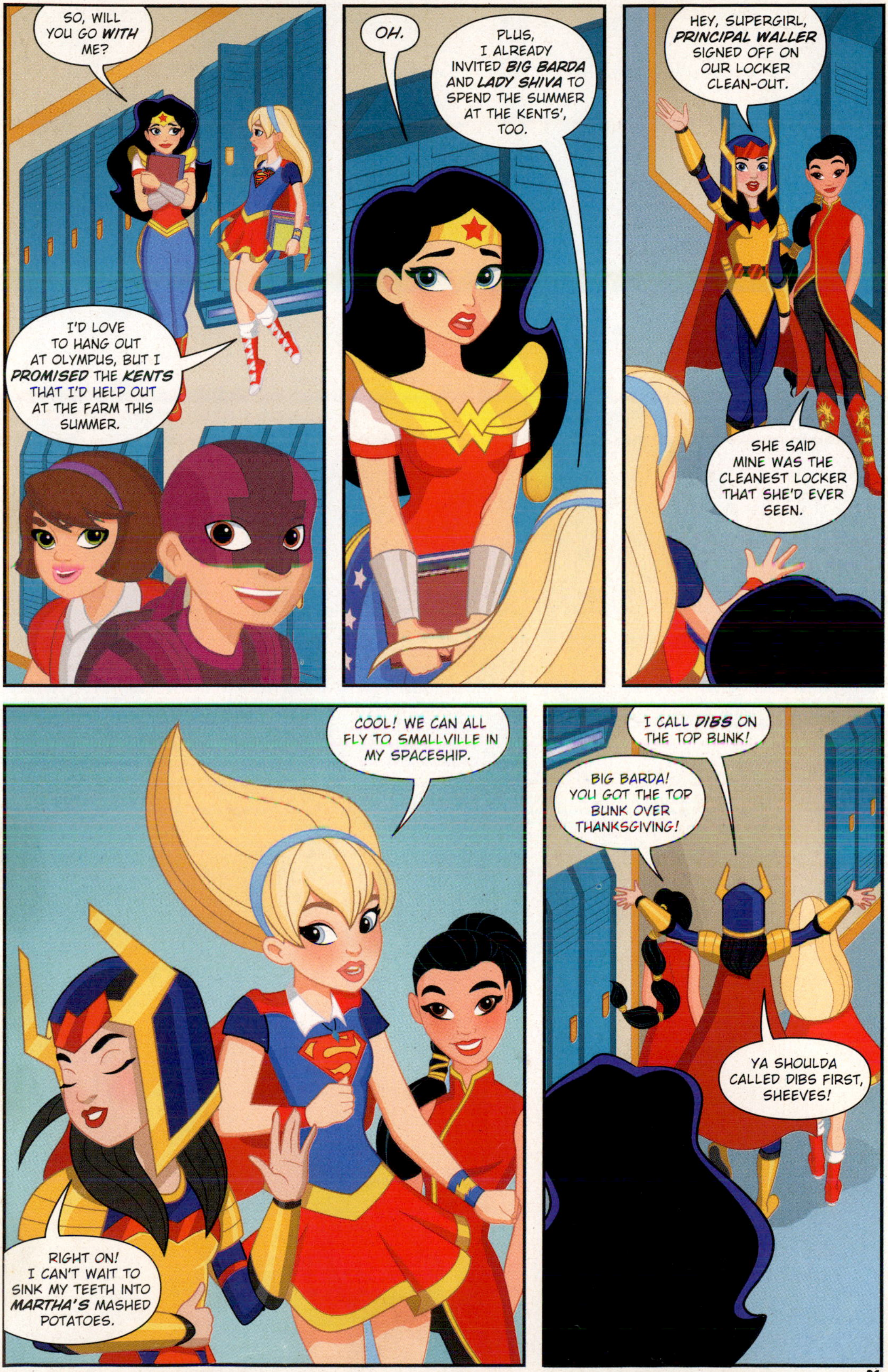
SO, WILL YOU GO WITH ME?
I'D LOVE TO HANG OUT AT OLYMPUS, BUT I PROMISED THE KENTS THAT I'D HELP OUT AT THE FARM THIS SUMMER.
OH.
PLUS, I ALREADY INVITED BIG BARDA AND LADY SHIVA TO SPEND THE SUMMER AT THE KENTS', TOO.
HEY, SUPERGIRL, PRINCIPAL WALLER SIGNED OFF ON OUR LOCKER CLEAN-OUT.
SHE SAID MINE WAS THE CLEANEST LOCKER THAT SHE'D EVER SEEN.
COOL! WE CAN ALL FLY TO SMALLVILLE IN MY SPACESHIP.
RIGHT ON! I CAN'T WAIT TO SINK MY TEETH INTO MARTHA'S MASHED POTATOES.
I CALL DIBS ON THE TOP BUNK!
BIG BARDA! YOU GOT THE TOP BUNK OVER THANKSGIVING!
YA SHOULDA CALLED DIBS FIRST, SHEEVES!

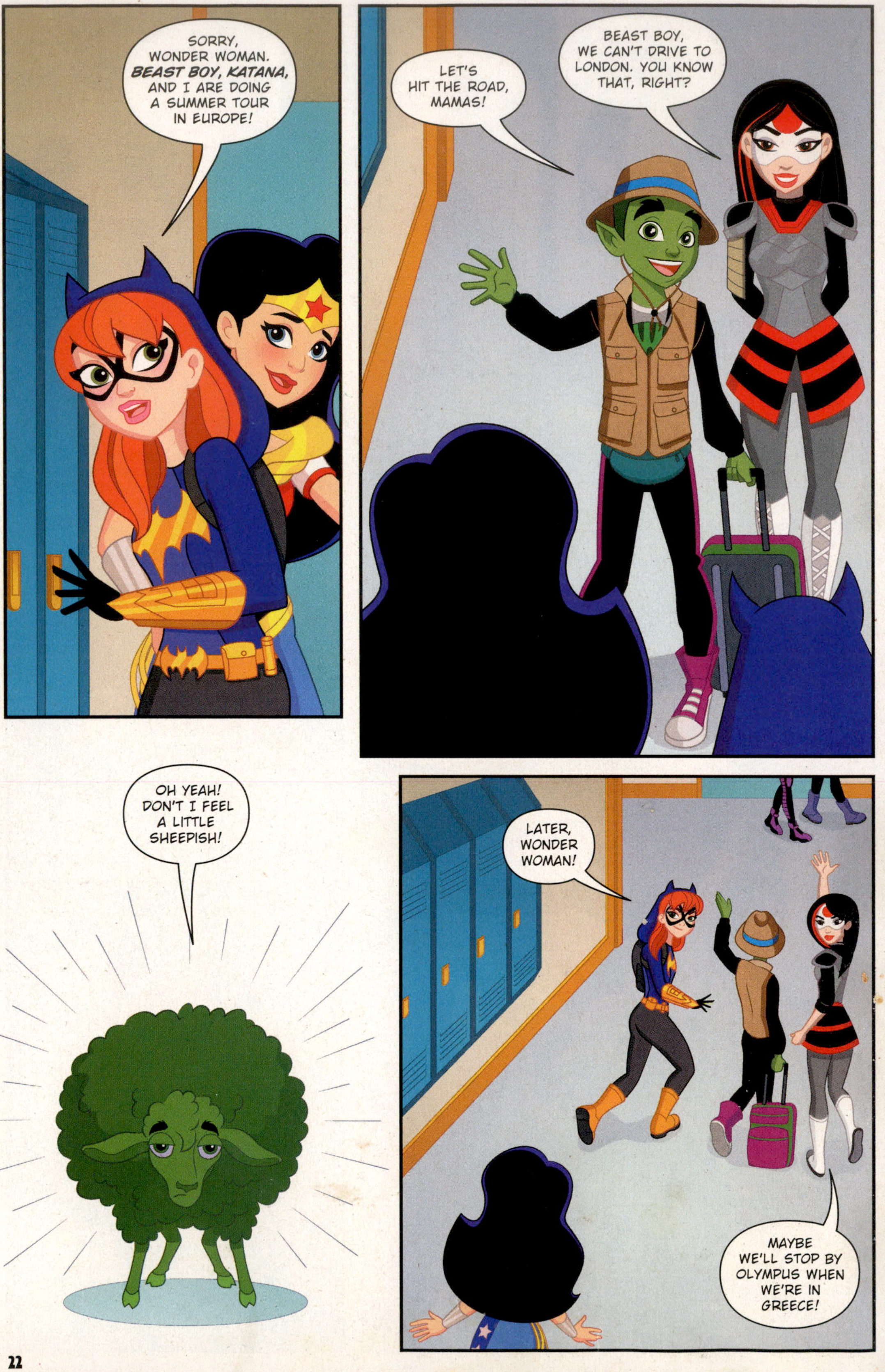

SORRY, WONDER WOMAN. BEAST BOY, KATANA, AND I ARE DOING A SUMMER TOUR IN EUROPE!
LET'S HIT THE ROAD, MAMAS!
BEAST BOY, WE CAN'T DRIVE TO LONDON. YOU KNOW THAT, RIGHT?
OH YEAH! DON'T I FEEL A LITTLE SHEEPISH!
LATER, WONDER WOMAN!
MAYBE WE'LL STOP BY OLYMPUS WHEN WE'RE IN GREECE!

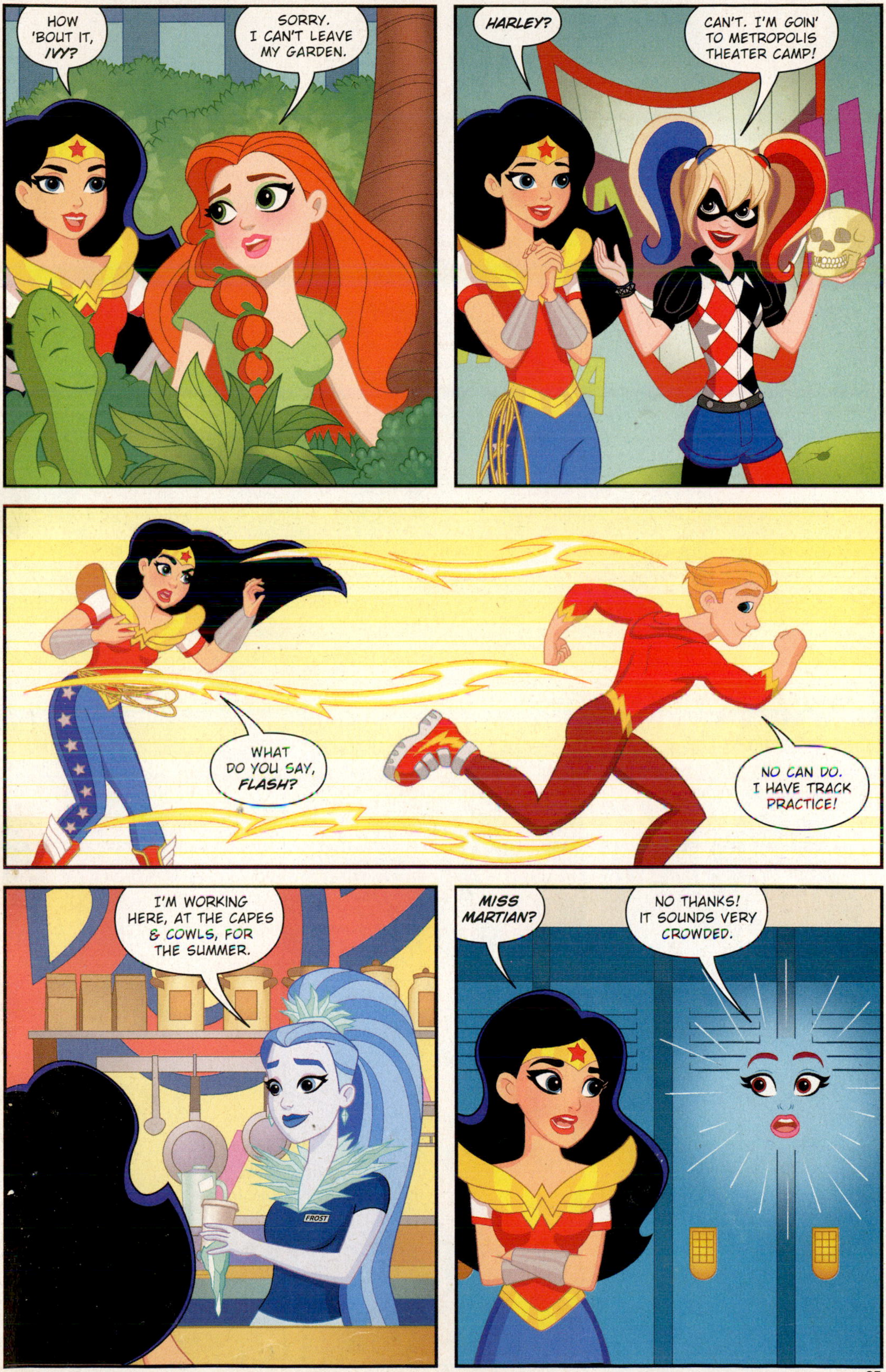
HOW 'BOUT IT, IVY?
SORRY. I CAN'T LEAVE MY GARDEN.
HARLEY?
CAN'T. I'M GOIN' TO METROPOLIS THEATER CAMP!
WHAT DO YOU SAY, FLASH?
NO CAN DO. I HAVE TRACK PRACTICE!
I'M WORKING HERE, AT THE CAPES & COWLS, FOR THE SUMMER.
FROST
MISS MARTIAN?
NO THANKS! IT SOUNDS VERY CROWDED.

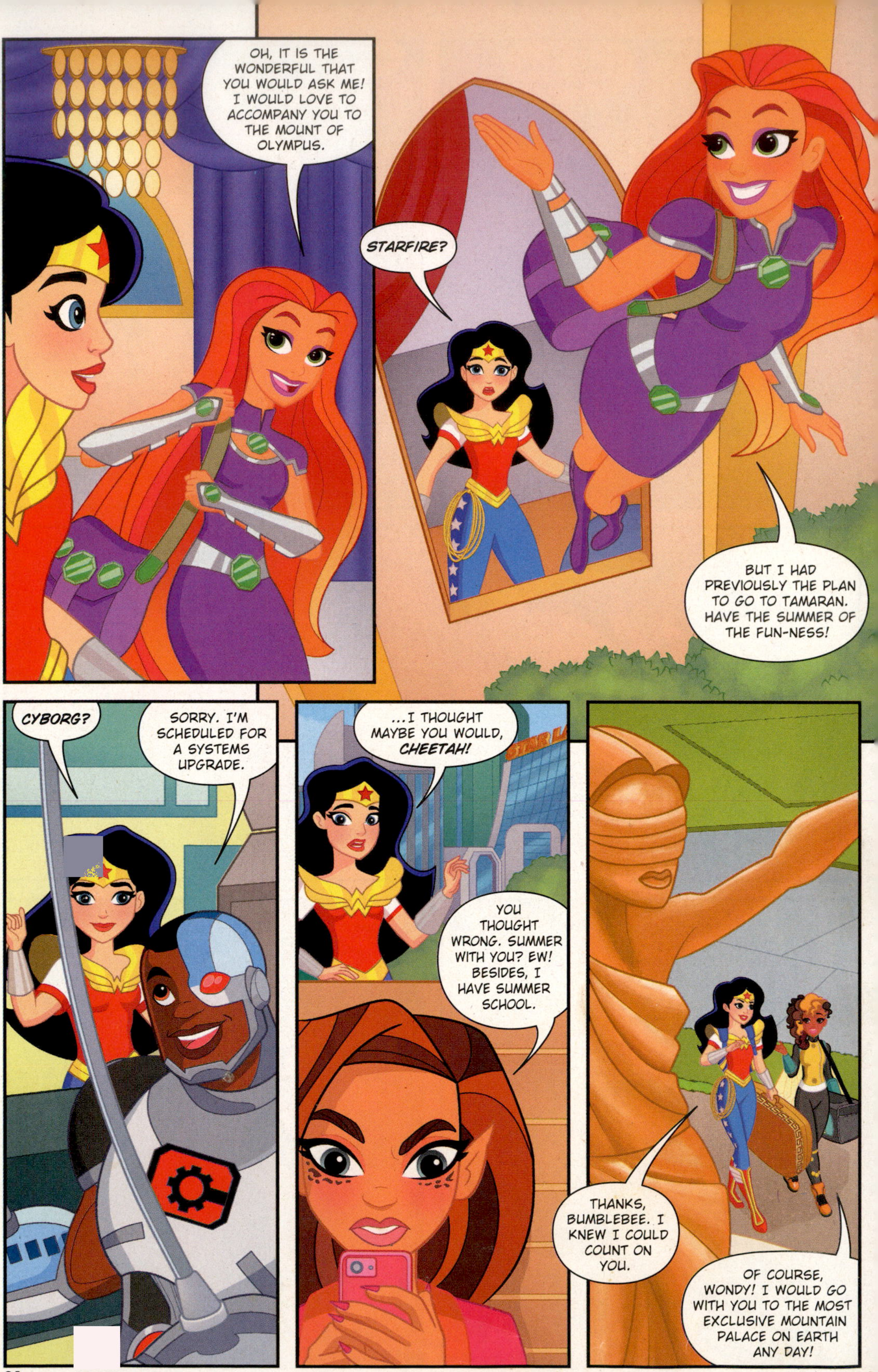
OH, IT IS THE WONDERFUL THAT YOU WOULD ASK ME! I WOULD LOVE TO ACCOMPANY YOU TO THE MOUNT OF OLYMPUS.
STARFIRE?
BUT I HAD PREVIOUSLY THE PLAN TO GO TO TAMARAN. HAVE THE SUMMER OF THE FUN-NESS!
CYBORG?
SORRY. I'M SCHEDULED FOR A SYSTEMS UPGRADE.
...I THOUGHT MAYBE YOU WOULD, CHEETAH!
YOU THOUGHT WRONG. SUMMER WITH YOU? EW! BESIDES, I HAVE SUMMER SCHOOL.
THANKS, BUMBLEBEE. I KNEW I COULD COUNT ON YOU.
OF COURSE, WONDY! I WOULD GO WITH YOU TO THE MOST EXCLUSIVE MOUNTAIN PALACE ON EARTH ANY DAY!

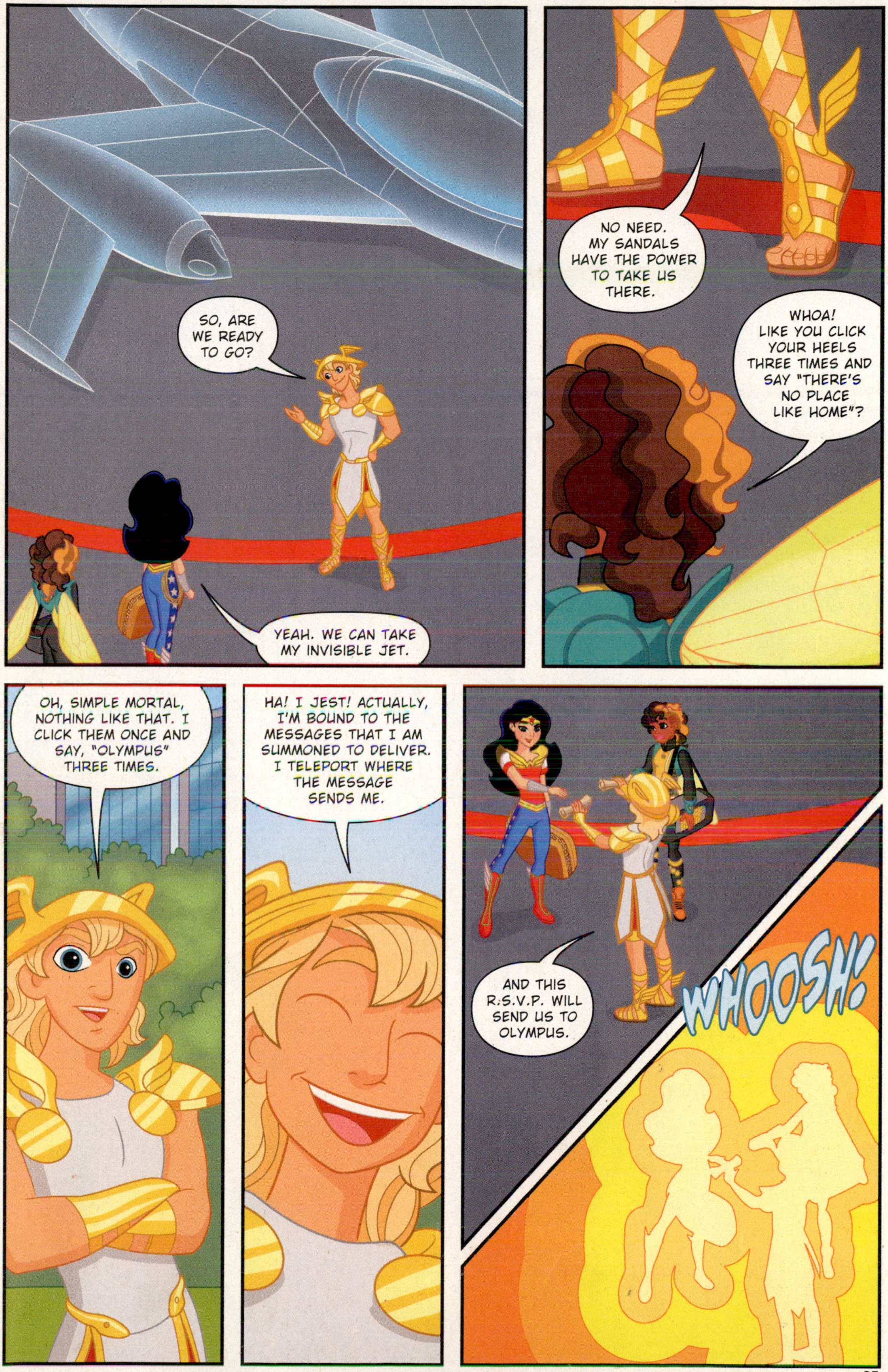

SO, ARE WE READY TO GO?
YEAH. WE CAN TAKE MY INVISIBLE JET.
NO NEED. MY SANDALS HAVE THE POWER TO TAKE US THERE.
WHOA! LIKE YOU CLICK YOUR HEELS THREE TIMES AND SAY "THERE'S NO PLACE LIKE HOME"?
OH, SIMPLE MORTAL, NOTHING LIKE THAT. I CLICK THEM ONCE AND SAY, "OLYMPUS" THREE TIMES.
HA! I JEST! ACTUALLY, I'M BOUND TO THE MESSAGES THAT I AM SUMMONED TO DELIVER. I TELEPORT WHERE THE MESSAGE SENDS ME.
AND THIS R.S.V.P. WILL SEND US TO OLYMPUS.
WHOOSH!

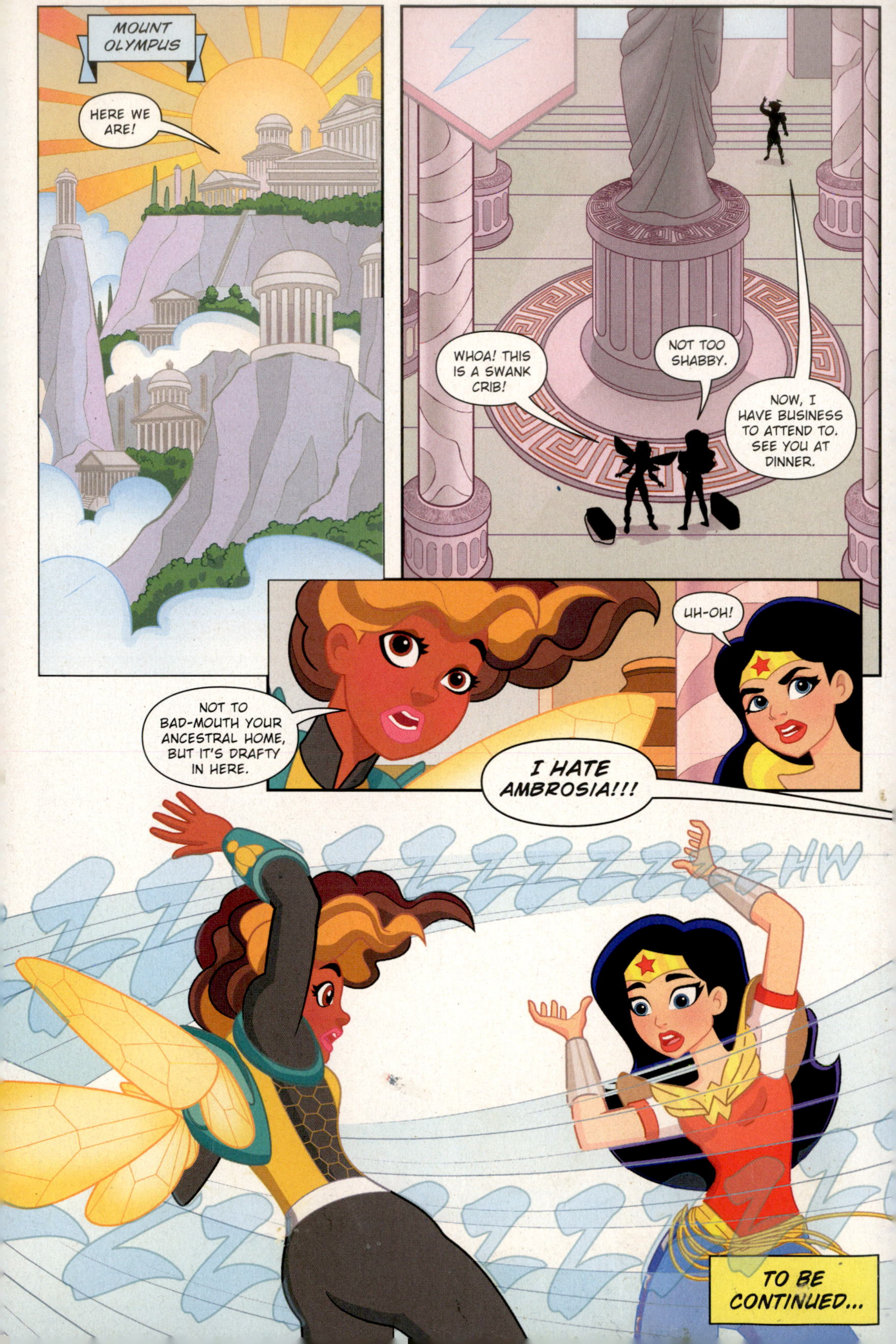
MOUNT OLYMPUS
HERE WE ARE!
WHOA! THIS IS A SWANK CRIB!
NOT TOO SHABBY.
NOW, I HAVE BUSINESS TO ATTEND TO. SEE YOU AT DINNER.
NOT TO BAD-MOUTH YOUR ANCESTRAL HOME, BUT IT'S DRAFTY IN HERE.
UH-OH!
I HATE AMBROSIA!!!
ZZZZZZZZZZZZHW
TO BE CONTINUED...

CHAPTER TWO
SUMMERTIME MADNESS

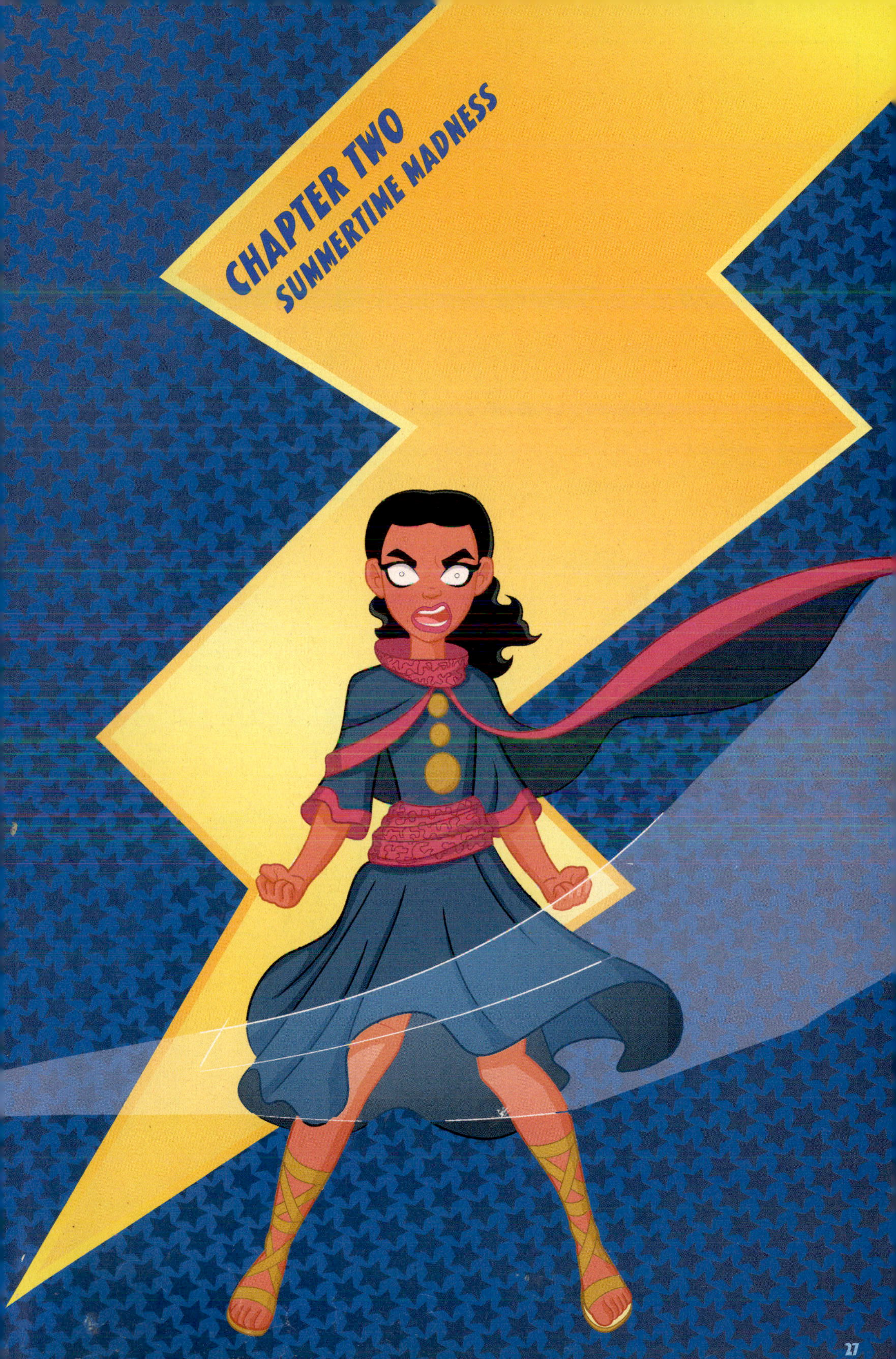

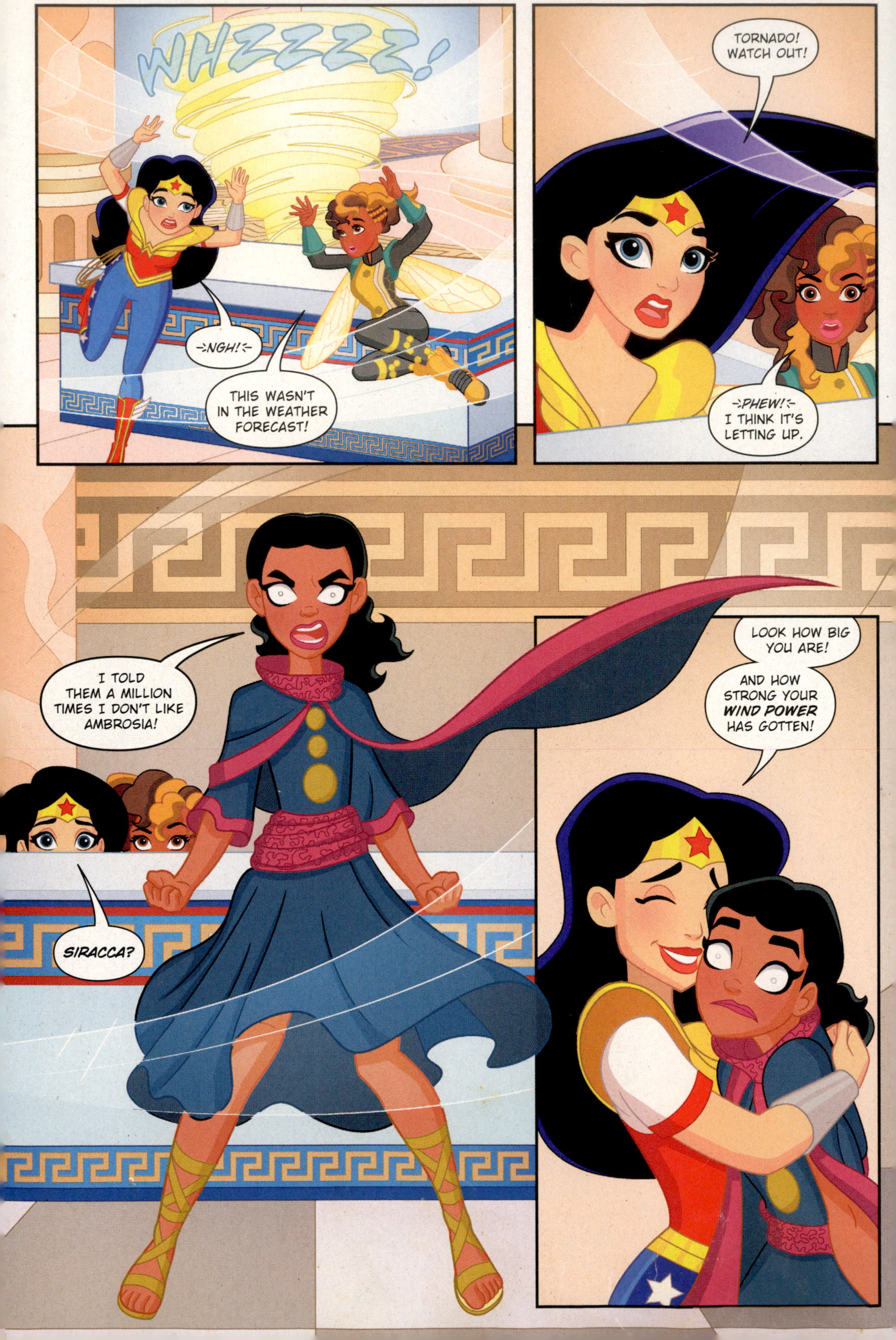
WHZZZZZ!
-NGH!-
THIS WASN'T IN THE WEATHER FORECAST!
TORNADO! WATCH OUT!
-PHEW!- I THINK IT'S LETTING UP.
I TOLD THEM A MILLION TIMES I DON'T LIKE AMBROSIA!
SIRACCA?
LOOK HOW BIG YOU ARE!
AND HOW STRONG YOUR **WIND POWER** HAS GOTTEN!

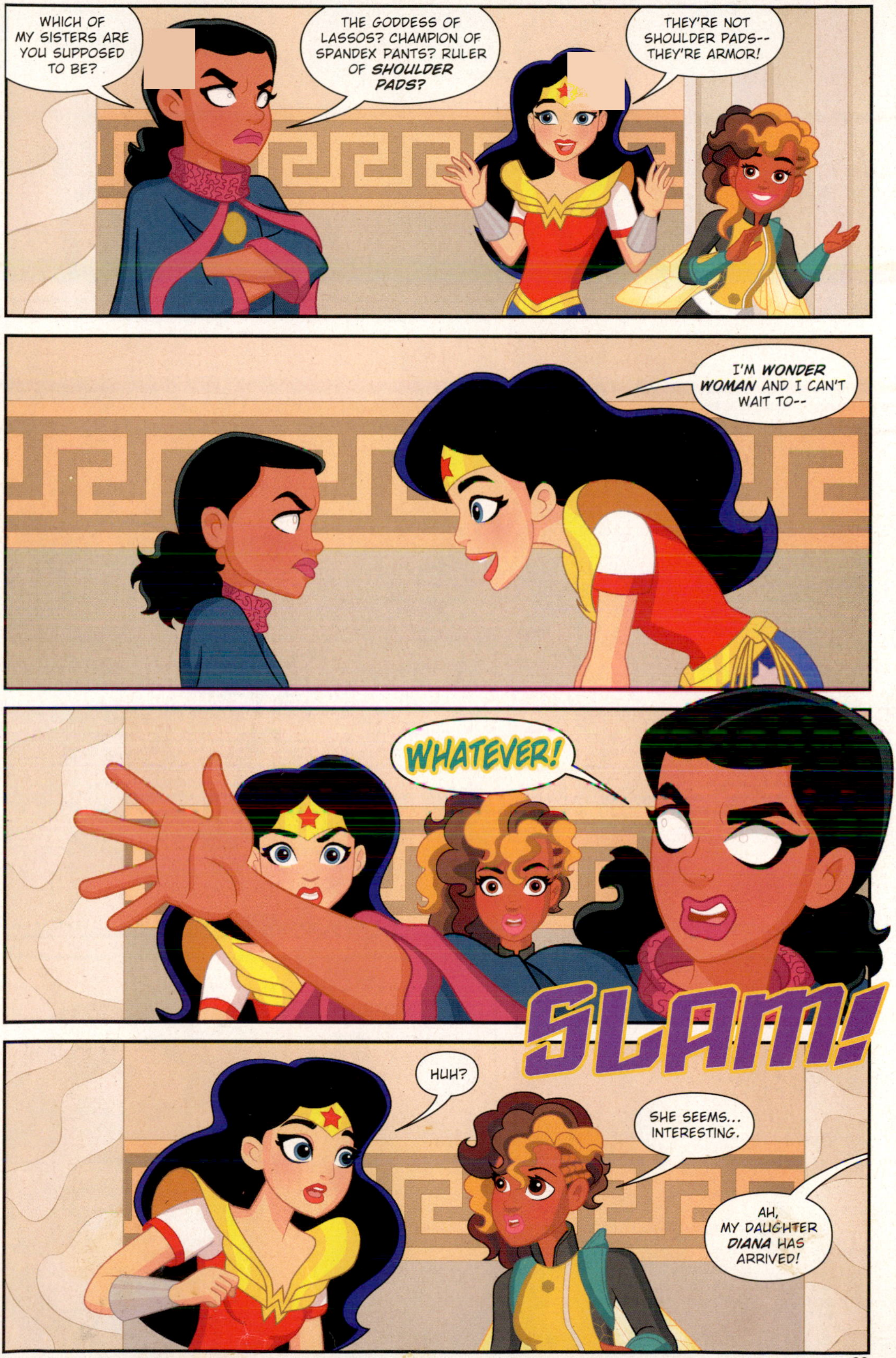
WHICH OF MY SISTERS ARE YOU SUPPOSED TO BE?
THE GODDESS OF LASSOS? CHAMPION OF SPANDEX PANTS? RULER OF SHOULDER PADS?
THEY'RE NOT SHOULDER PADS-- THEY'RE ARMOR!
I'M WONDER WOMAN AND I CAN'T WAIT TO--
WHATEVER!
SLAM!
HUH?
SHE SEEMS... INTERESTING.
AH, MY DAUGHTER DIANA HAS ARRIVED!

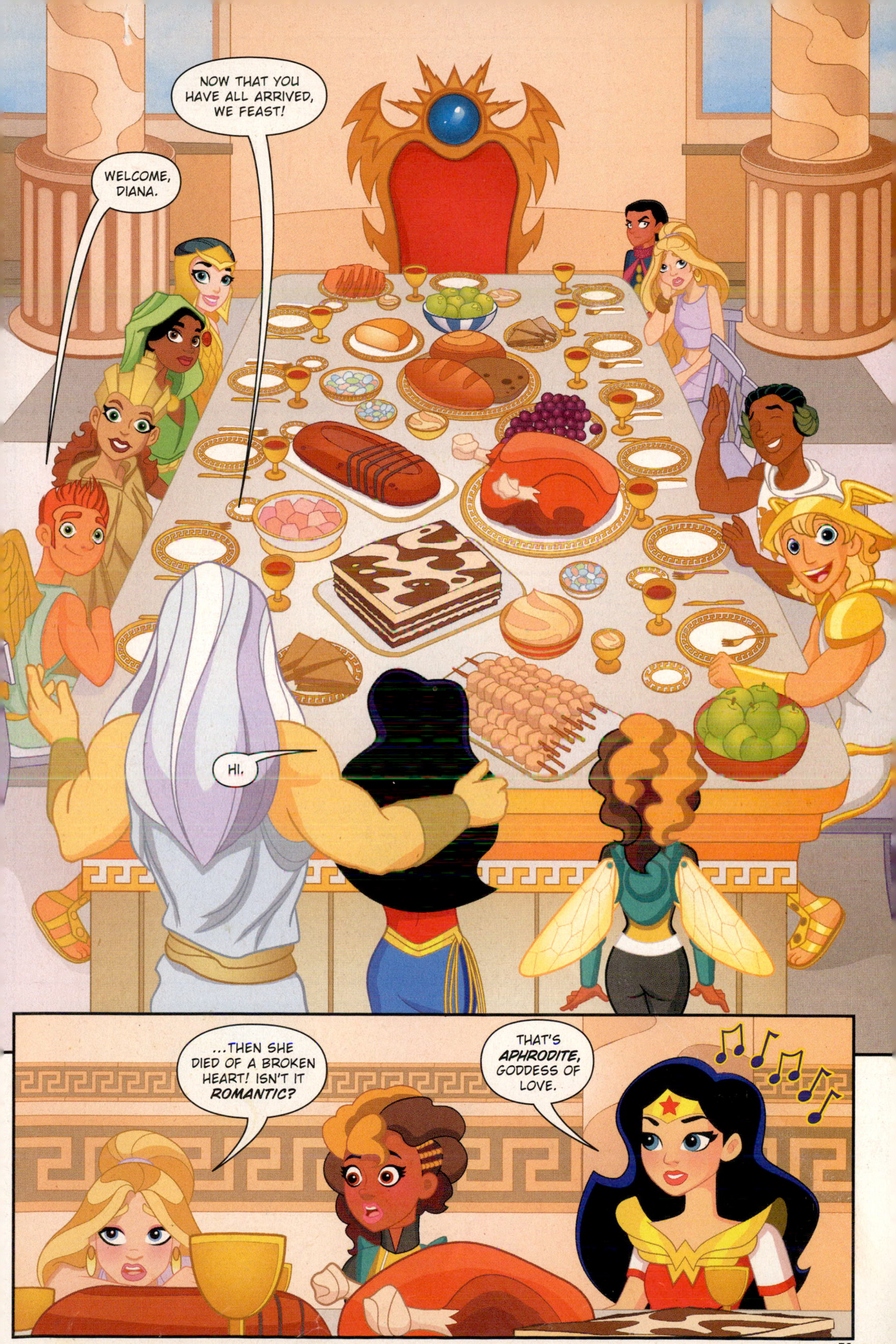

NOW THAT YOU HAVE ALL ARRIVED, WE FEAST!
WELCOME, DIANA.
HI.
...THEN SHE DIED OF A BROKEN HEART! ISN'T IT ROMANTIC?
THAT'S APHRODITE, GODDESS OF LOVE.

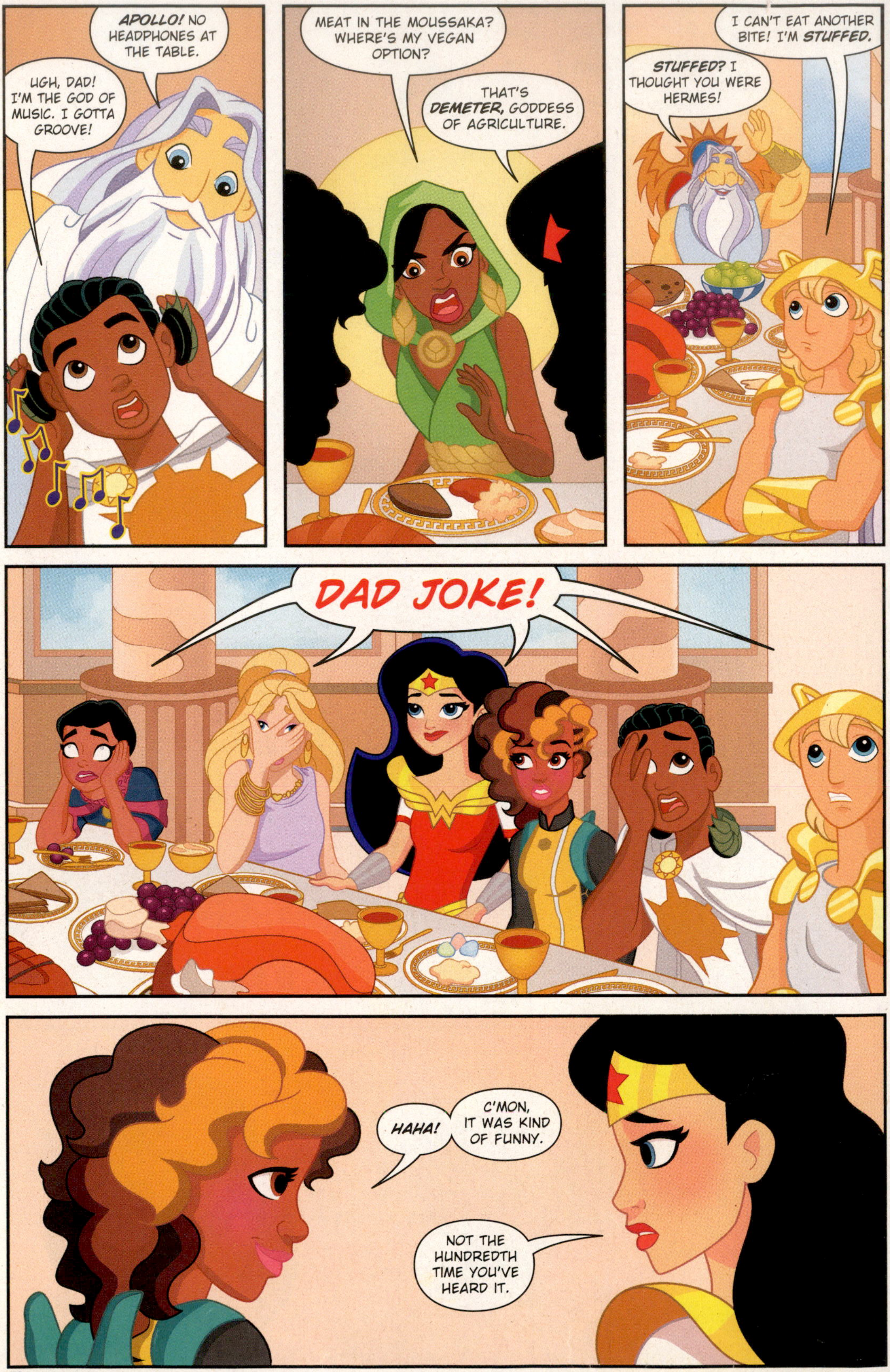
APOLLO! NO HEADPHONES AT THE TABLE.
UGH, DAD! I'M THE GOD OF MUSIC. I GOTTA GROOVE!
MEAT IN THE MOUSSAKA? WHERE'S MY VEGAN OPTION?
THAT'S DEMETER, GODDESS OF AGRICULTURE.
I CAN'T EAT ANOTHER BITE! I'M STUFFED.
STUFFED? I THOUGHT YOU WERE HERMES!
DAD JOKE!
HAHA!
C'MON, IT WAS KIND OF FUNNY.
NOT THE HUNDREDTH TIME YOU'VE HEARD IT.

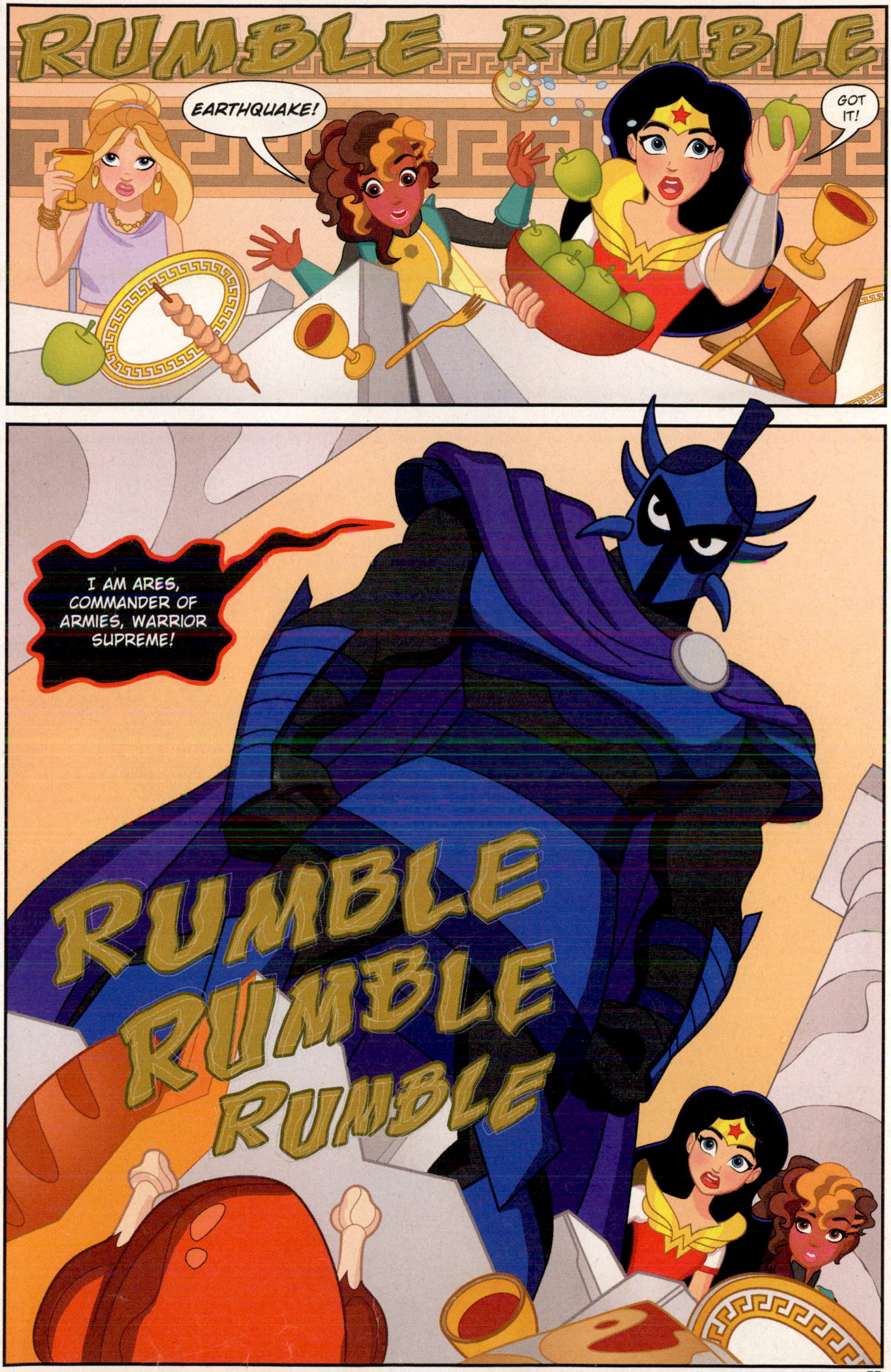
RUMBLE RUMBLE
EARTHQUAKE!
GOT IT!
I AM ARES, COMMANDER OF ARMIES, WARRIOR SUPREME!
RUMBLE
RUMBLE
RUMBLE

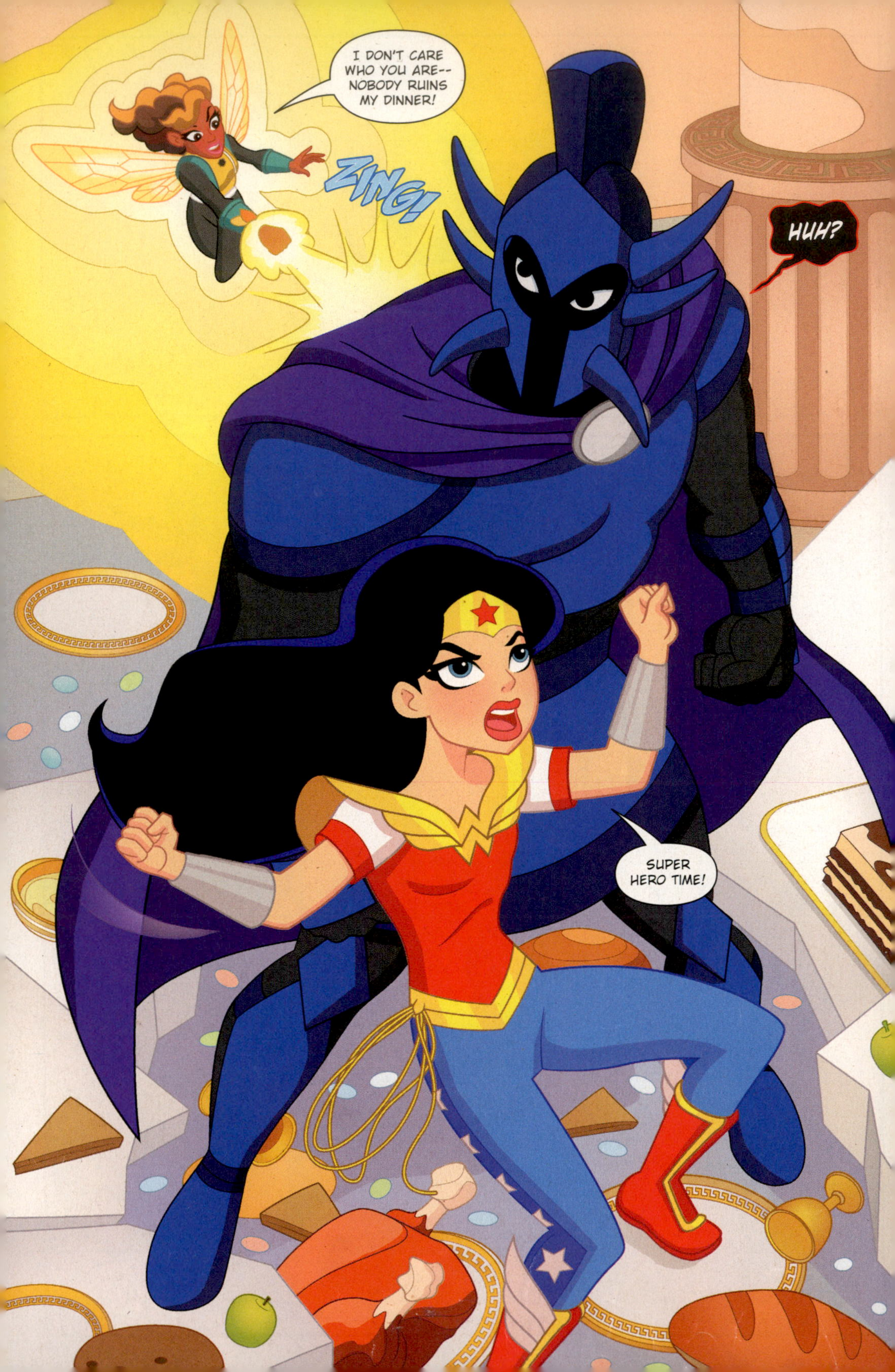
I DON'T CARE WHO YOU ARE-- NOBODY RUINS MY DINNER!
ZING!
HUH?
SUPER HERO TIME!

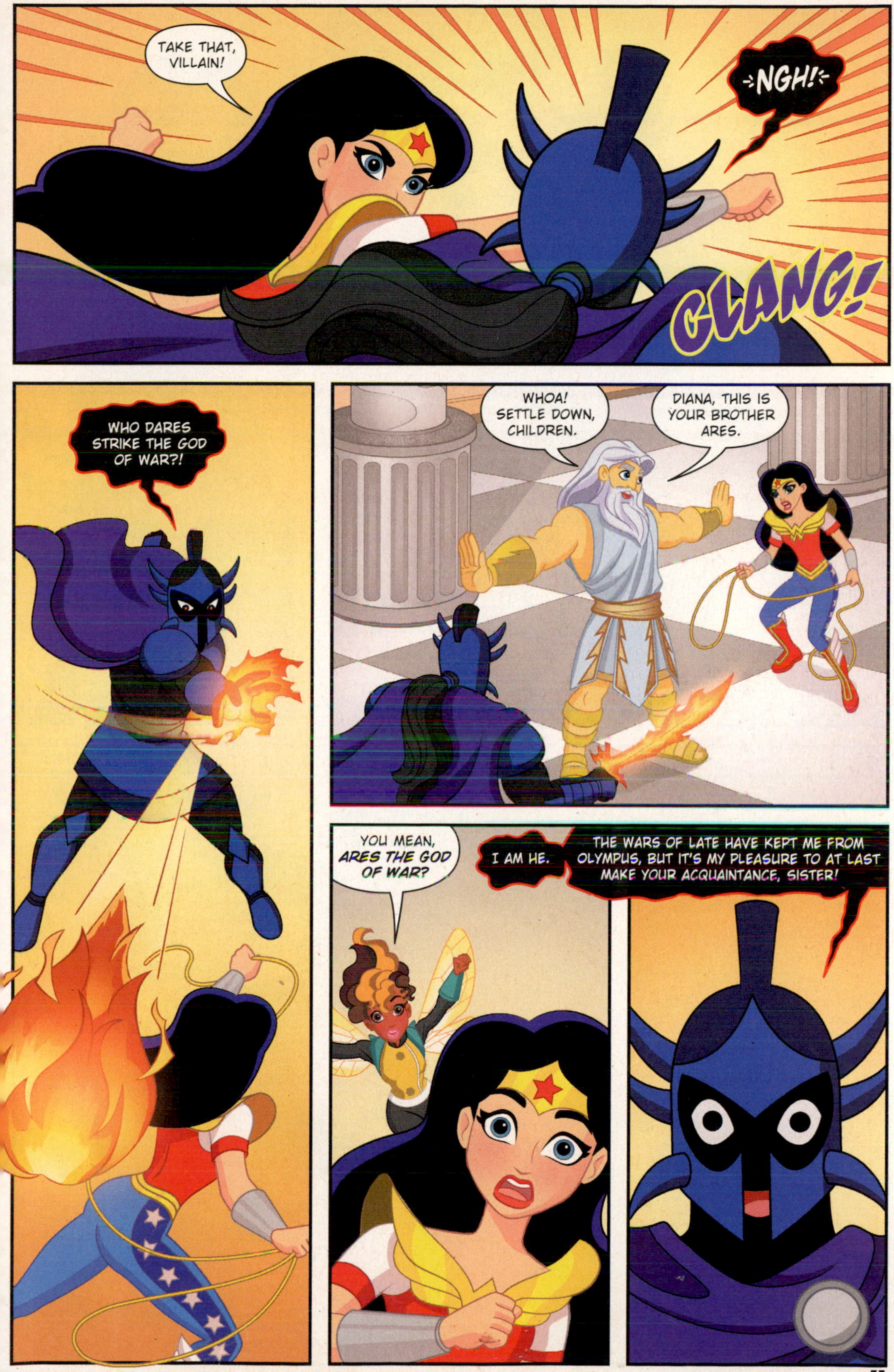
TAKE THAT, VILLAIN!
NGH!
CLANG!
WHO DARES STRIKE THE GOD OF WAR?!
WHOA! SETTLE DOWN, CHILDREN.
DIANA, THIS IS YOUR BROTHER ARES.
YOU MEAN, ARES THE GOD OF WAR?
I AM HE.
THE WARS OF LATE HAVE KEPT ME FROM OLYMPUS, BUT IT'S MY PLEASURE TO AT LAST MAKE YOUR ACQUAINTANCE, SISTER!

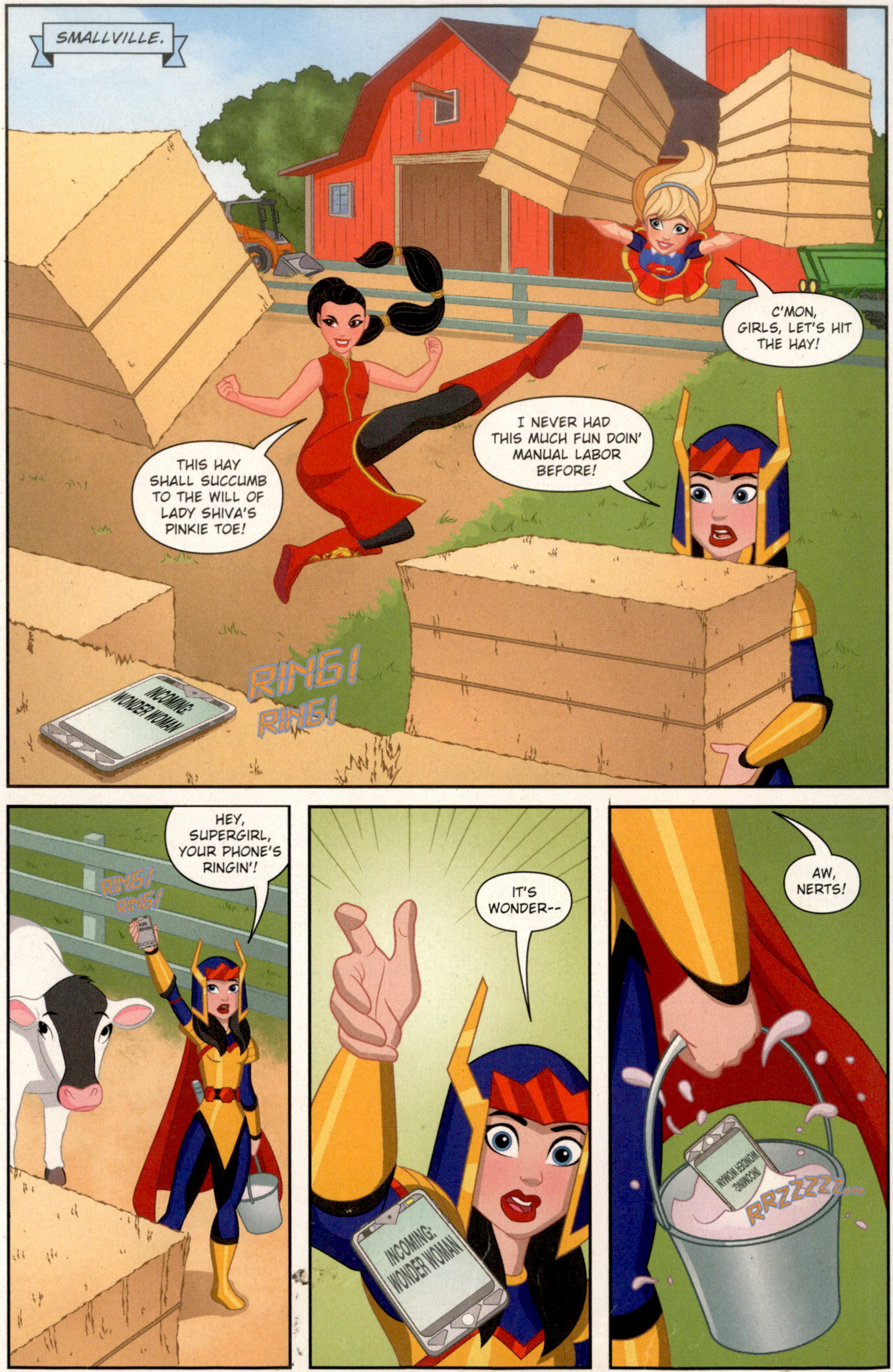
SMALLVILLE.
C'MON, GIRLS, LET'S HIT THE HAY!
I NEVER HAD THIS MUCH FUN DOIN' MANUAL LABOR BEFORE!
THIS HAY SHALL SUCCUMB TO THE WILL OF LADY SHIVA'S PINKIE TOE!
INCOMING: WONDER WOMAN
RING! RING!
HEY, SUPERGIRL, YOUR PHONE'S RINGIN'!
RING! RING!
IT'S WONDER--
INCOMING: WONDER WOMAN
AW, NERTS!
INCOMING: WONDER WOMAN
RRZZZZZ...

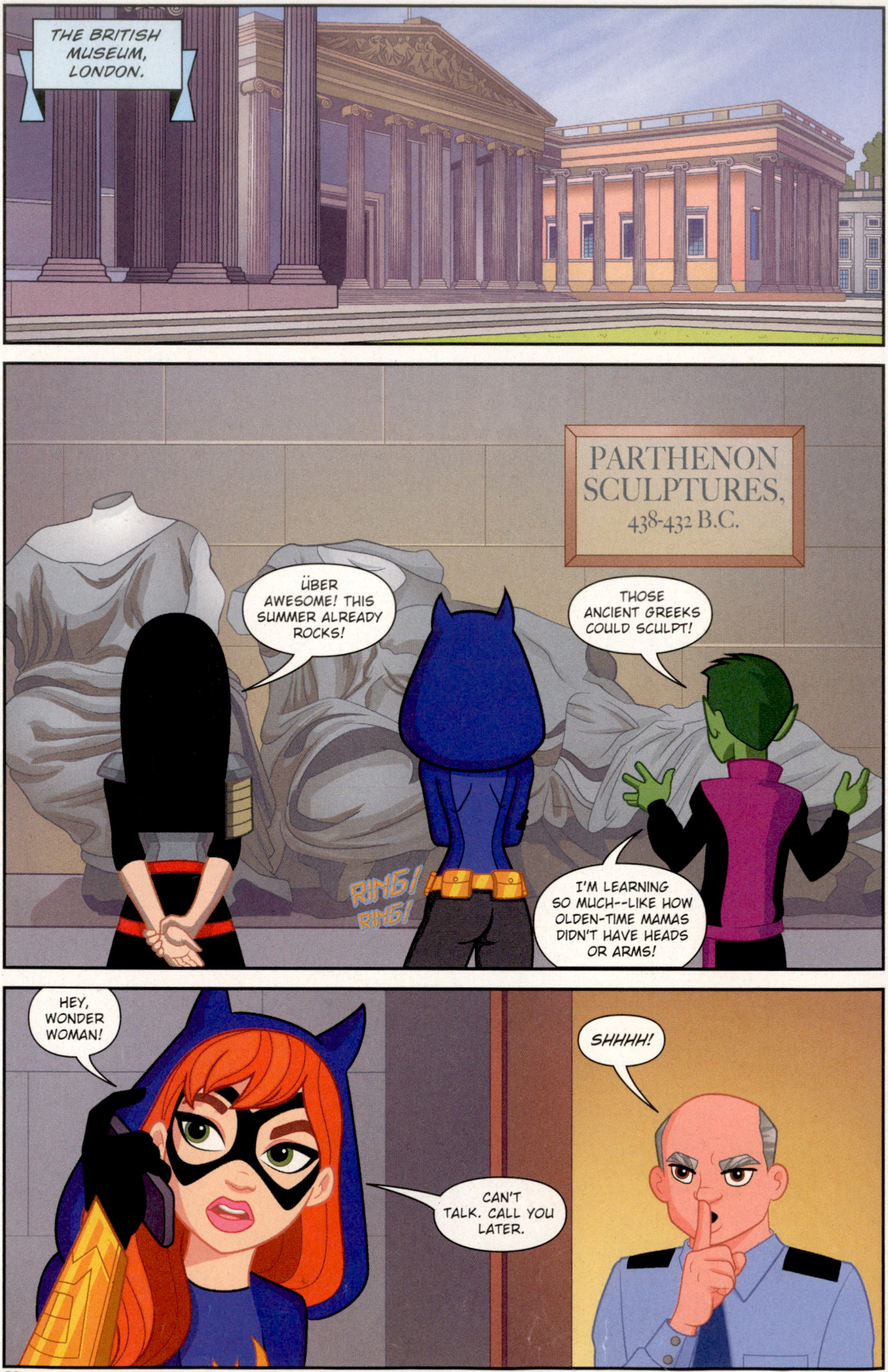
THE BRITISH MUSEUM, LONDON.
PARTHENON SCULPTURES, 438-432 B.C.
ÜBER AWESOME! THIS SUMMER ALREADY ROCKS!
THOSE ANCIENT GREEKS COULD SCULPT!
RING! RING!
I'M LEARNING SO MUCH--LIKE HOW OLDEN-TIME MAMAS DIDN'T HAVE HEADS OR ARMS!
HEY, WONDER WOMAN!
SHHHH!
CAN'T TALK. CALL YOU LATER.

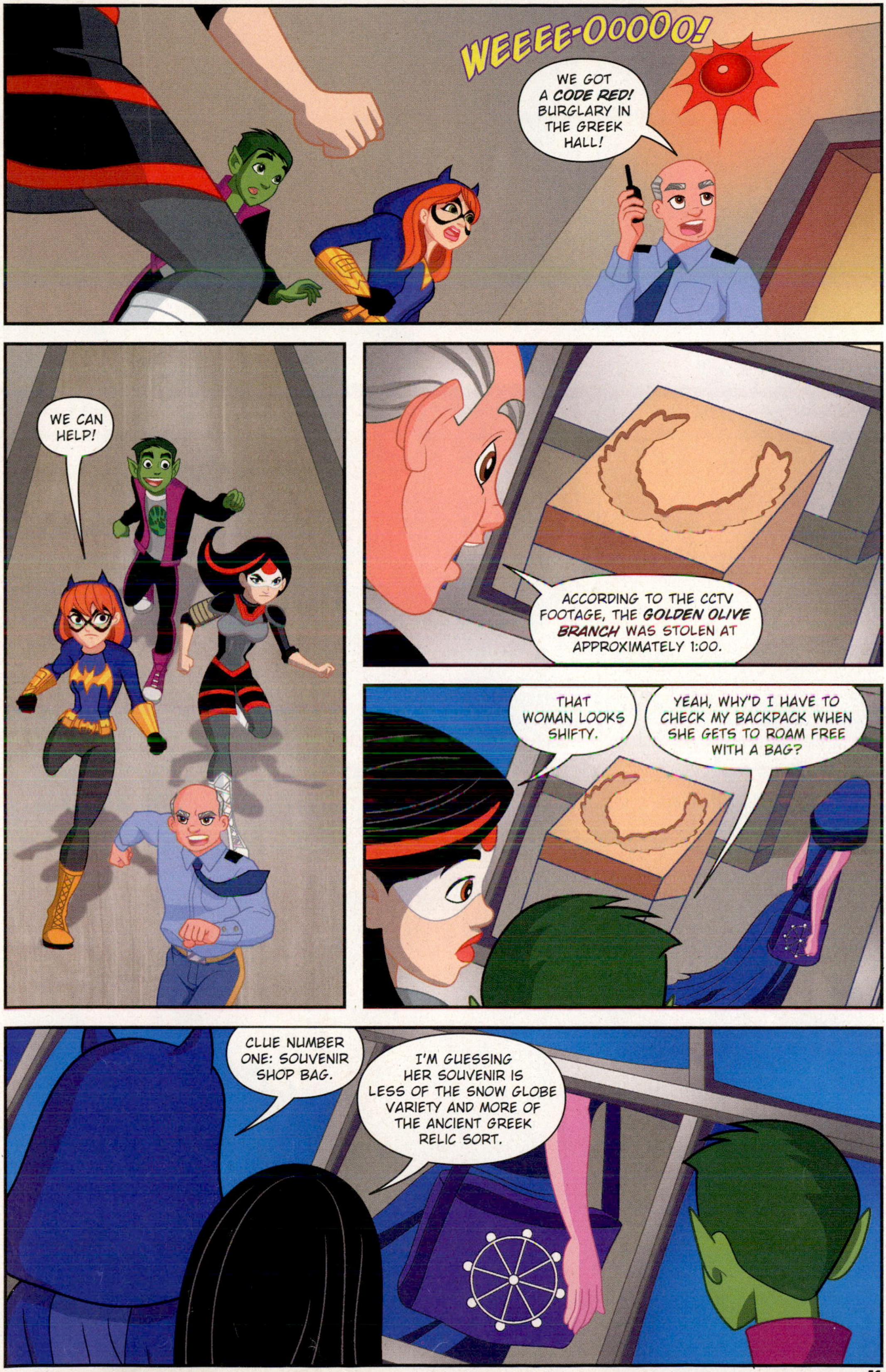
WEEEE-OOOOO!
WE GOT A CODE RED! BURGLARY IN THE GREEK HALL!
WE CAN HELP!
ACCORDING TO THE CCTV FOOTAGE, THE GOLDEN OLIVE BRANCH WAS STOLEN AT APPROXIMATELY 1:00.
THAT WOMAN LOOKS SHIFTY.
YEAH, WHY'D I HAVE TO CHECK MY BACKPACK WHEN SHE GETS TO ROAM FREE WITH A BAG?
CLUE NUMBER ONE: SOUVENIR SHOP BAG.
I'M GUESSING HER SOUVENIR IS LESS OF THE SNOW GLOBE VARIETY AND MORE OF THE ANCIENT GREEK RELIC SORT.

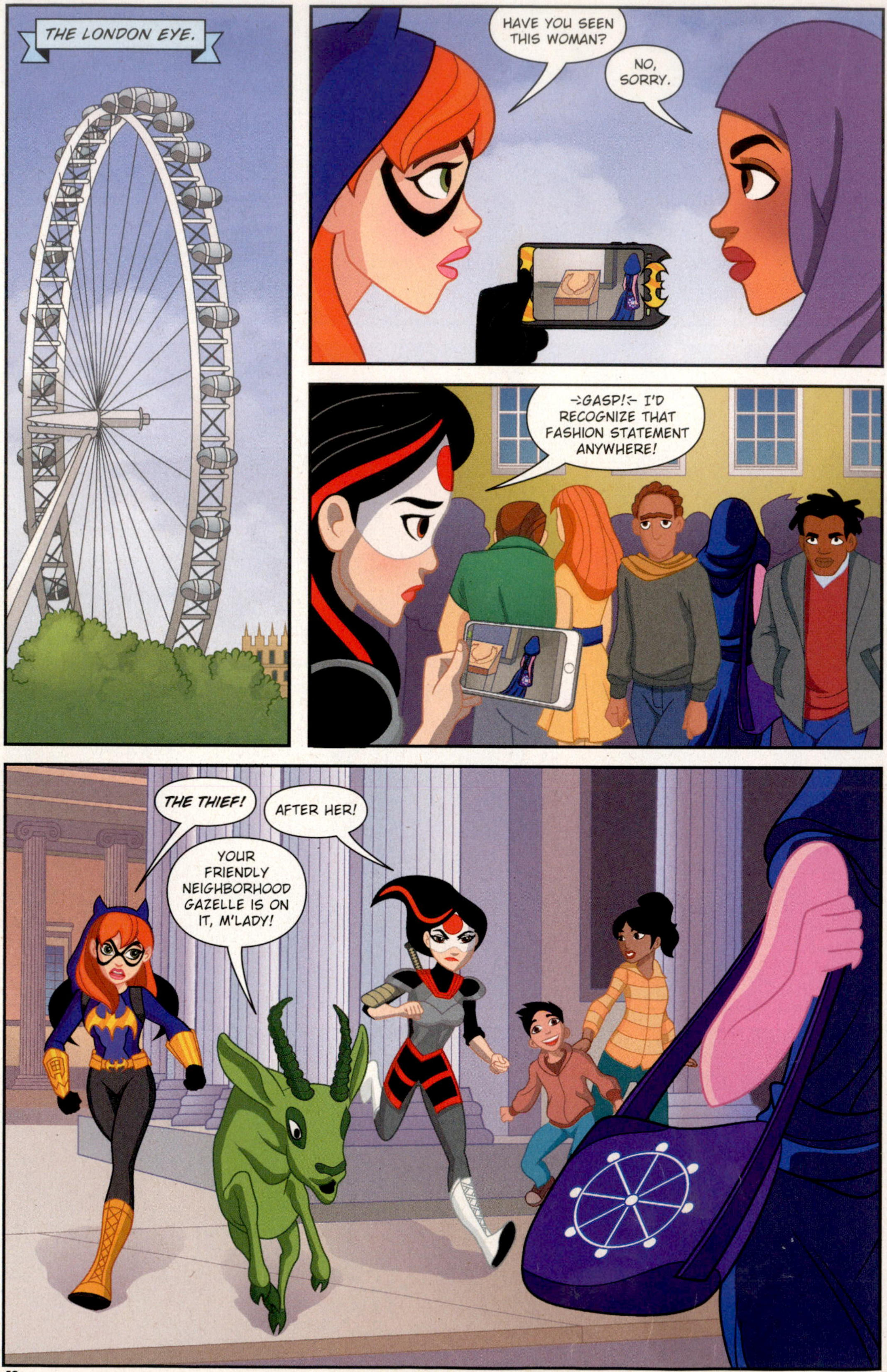
THE LONDON EYE.
HAVE YOU SEEN THIS WOMAN?
NO, SORRY.
-GASP!- I'D RECOGNIZE THAT FASHION STATEMENT ANYWHERE!
THE THIEF!
AFTER HER!
YOUR FRIENDLY NEIGHBORHOOD GAZELLE IS ON IT, M'LADY!

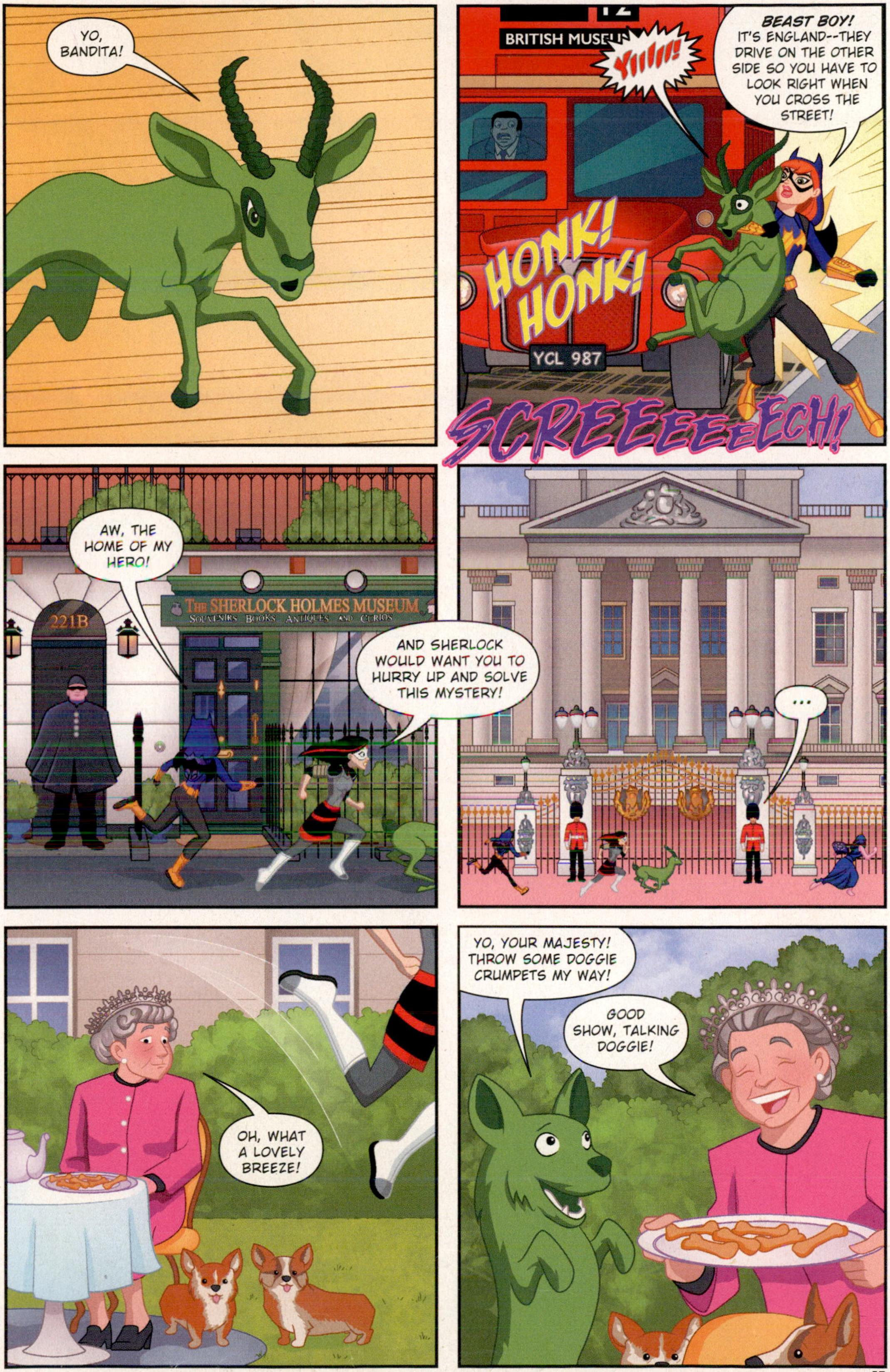
YO, BANDITA!
YIIII!!
BEAST BOY! IT'S ENGLAND--THEY DRIVE ON THE OTHER SIDE SO YOU HAVE TO LOOK RIGHT WHEN YOU CROSS THE STREET!
BRITISH MUSEU
HONK! HONK!
YCL 987
SCREEEEEEECH!
AW, THE HOME OF MY HERO!
221B
THE SHERLOCK HOLMES MUSEUM
SOUVENIRS BOOKS ANTIQUES AND CURIOS
AND SHERLOCK WOULD WANT YOU TO HURRY UP AND SOLVE THIS MYSTERY!
...
OH, WHAT A LOVELY BREEZE!
YO, YOUR MAJESTY! THROW SOME DOGGIE CRUMPETS MY WAY!
GOOD SHOW, TALKING DOGGIE!

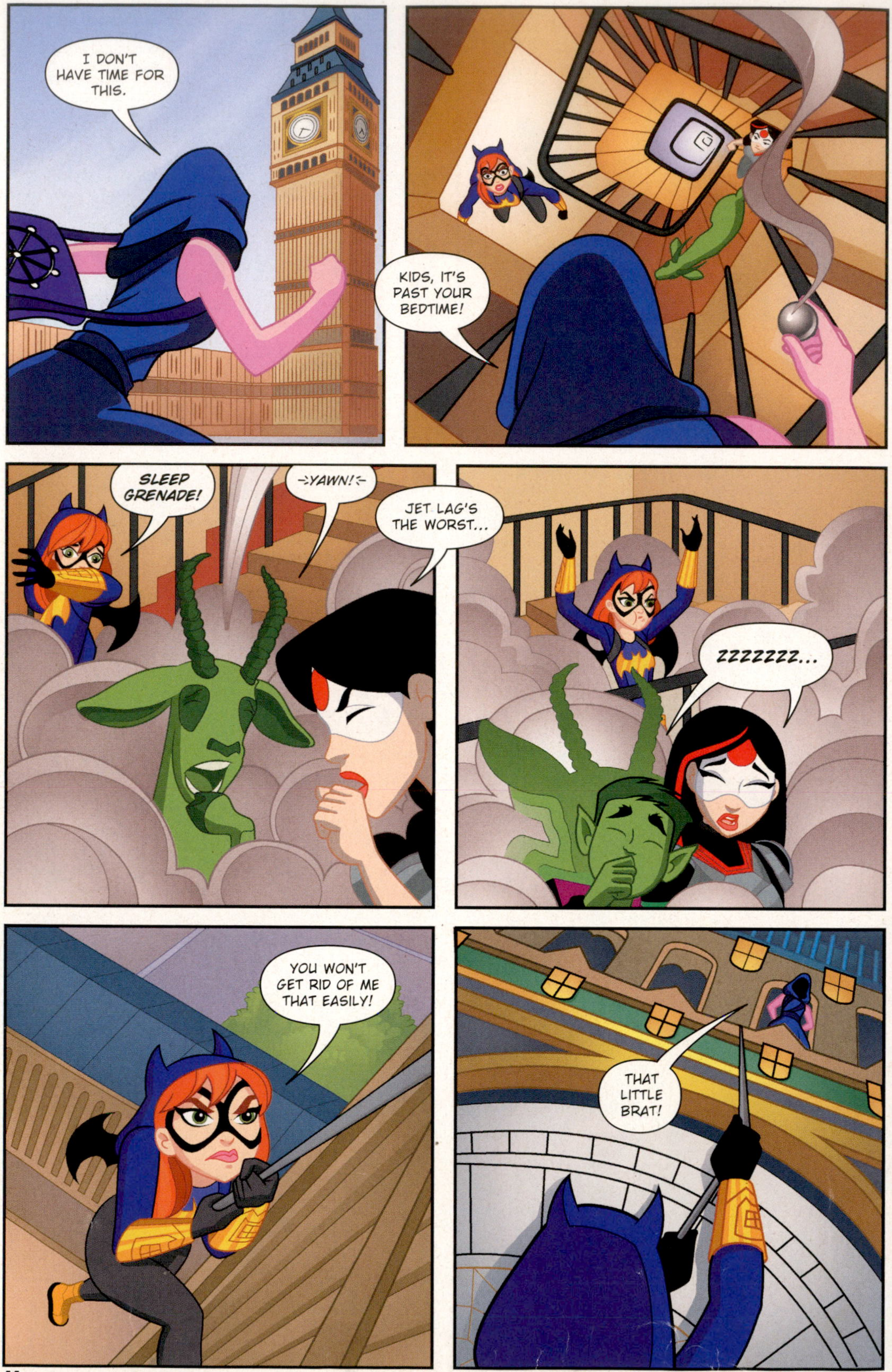
I DON'T HAVE TIME FOR THIS.
KIDS, IT'S PAST YOUR BEDTIME!
SLEEP GRENADE!
-YAWN!-
JET LAG'S THE WORST...
ZZZZZZZ...
YOU WON'T GET RID OF ME THAT EASILY!
THAT LITTLE BRAT!

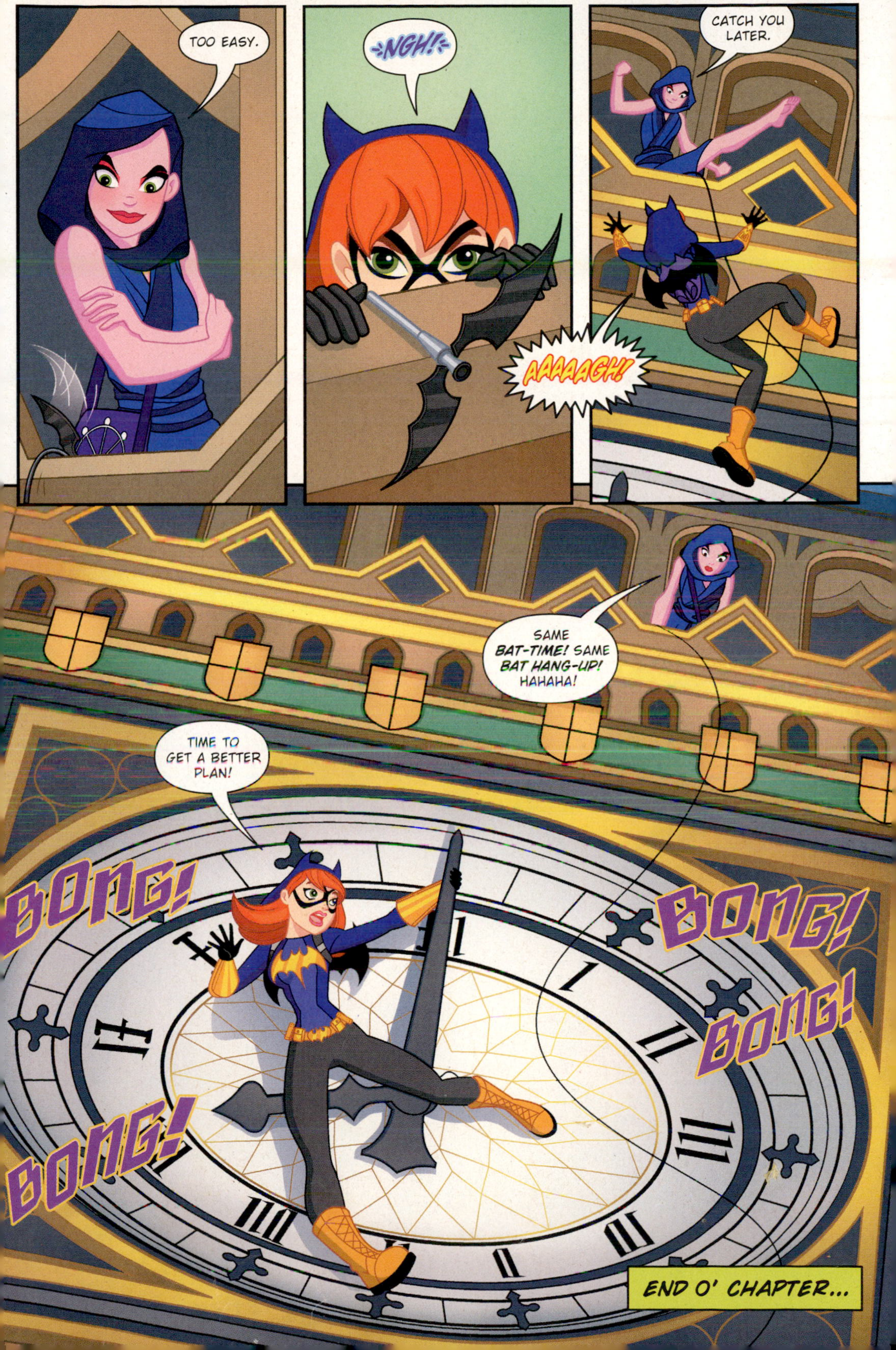
TOO EASY.
NGH!
CATCH YOU LATER.
AAAAAGH!
SAME BAT-TIME! SAME BAT HANG-UP! HAHAHA!
TIME TO GET A BETTER PLAN!
BONG!
BONG!
BONG!
BONG!
END O' CHAPTER...

CHAPTER THREE
FUN IN THE SUN

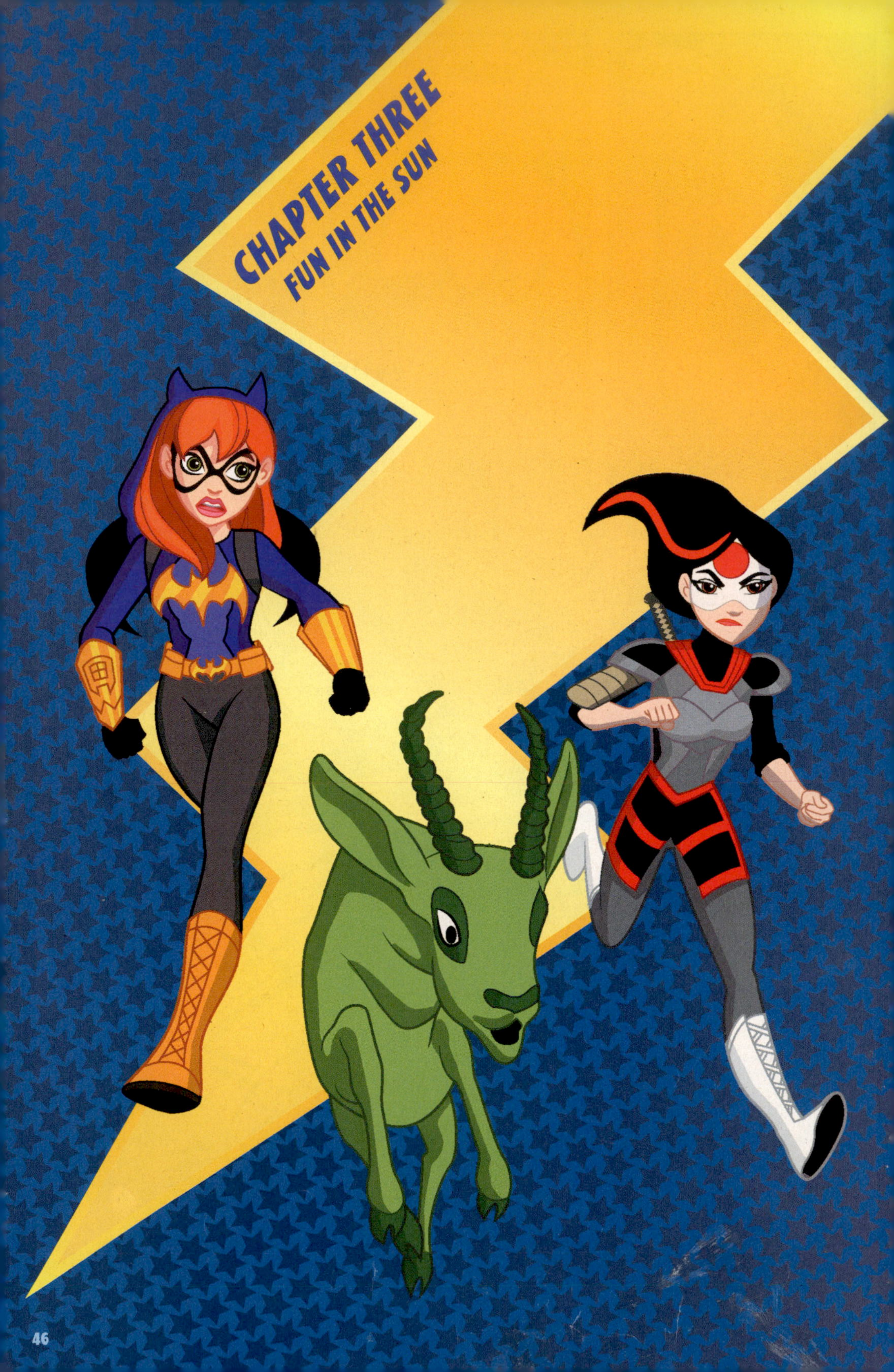

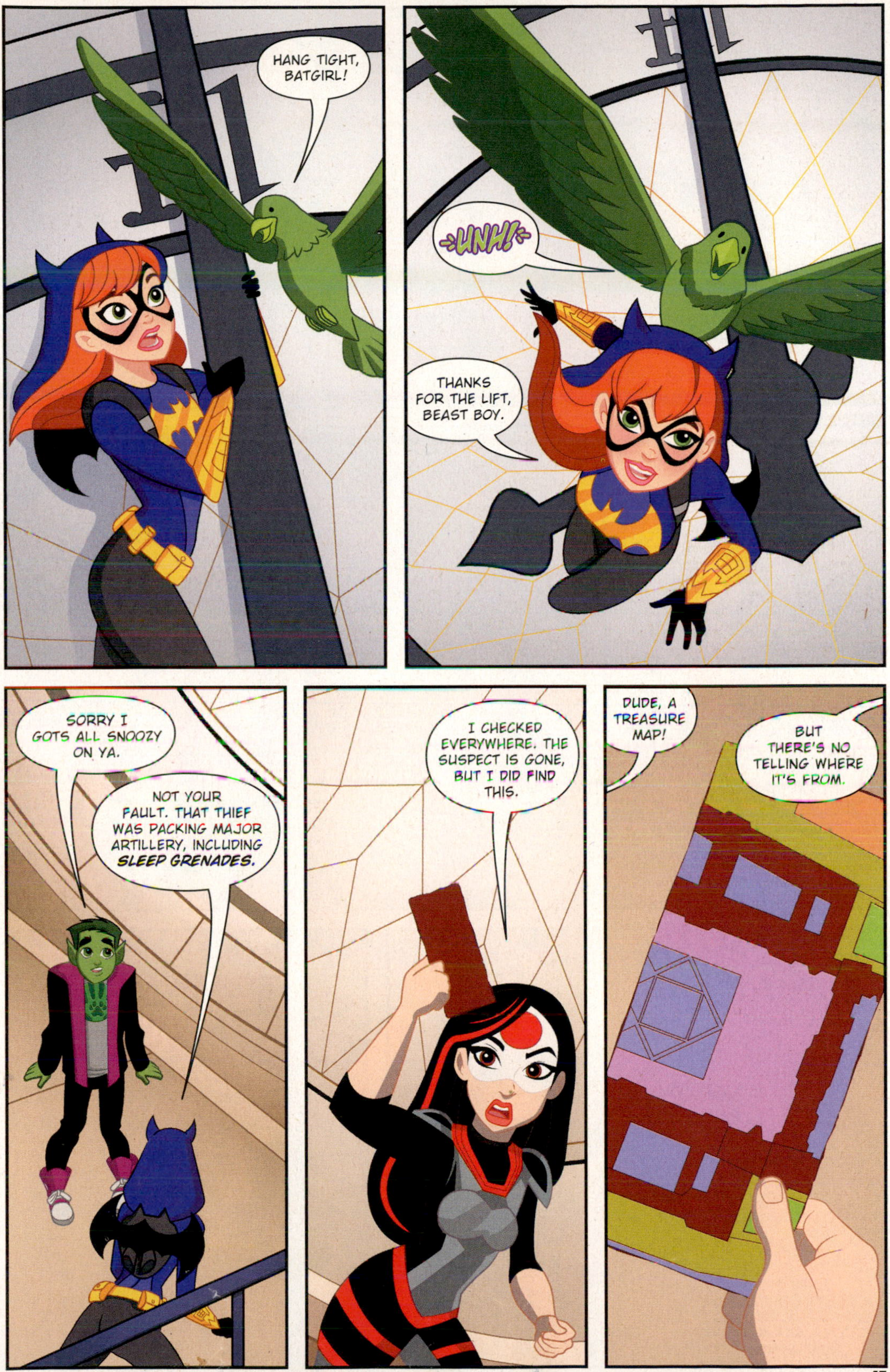
HANG TIGHT, BATGIRL!
UNH!
THANKS FOR THE LIFT, BEAST BOY.
SORRY I GOTS ALL SNOOZY ON YA.
NOT YOUR FAULT. THAT THIEF WAS PACKING MAJOR ARTILLERY, INCLUDING SLEEP GRENADES.
I CHECKED EVERYWHERE. THE SUSPECT IS GONE, BUT I DID FIND THIS.
DUDE, A TREASURE MAP!
BUT THERE'S NO TELLING WHERE IT'S FROM.

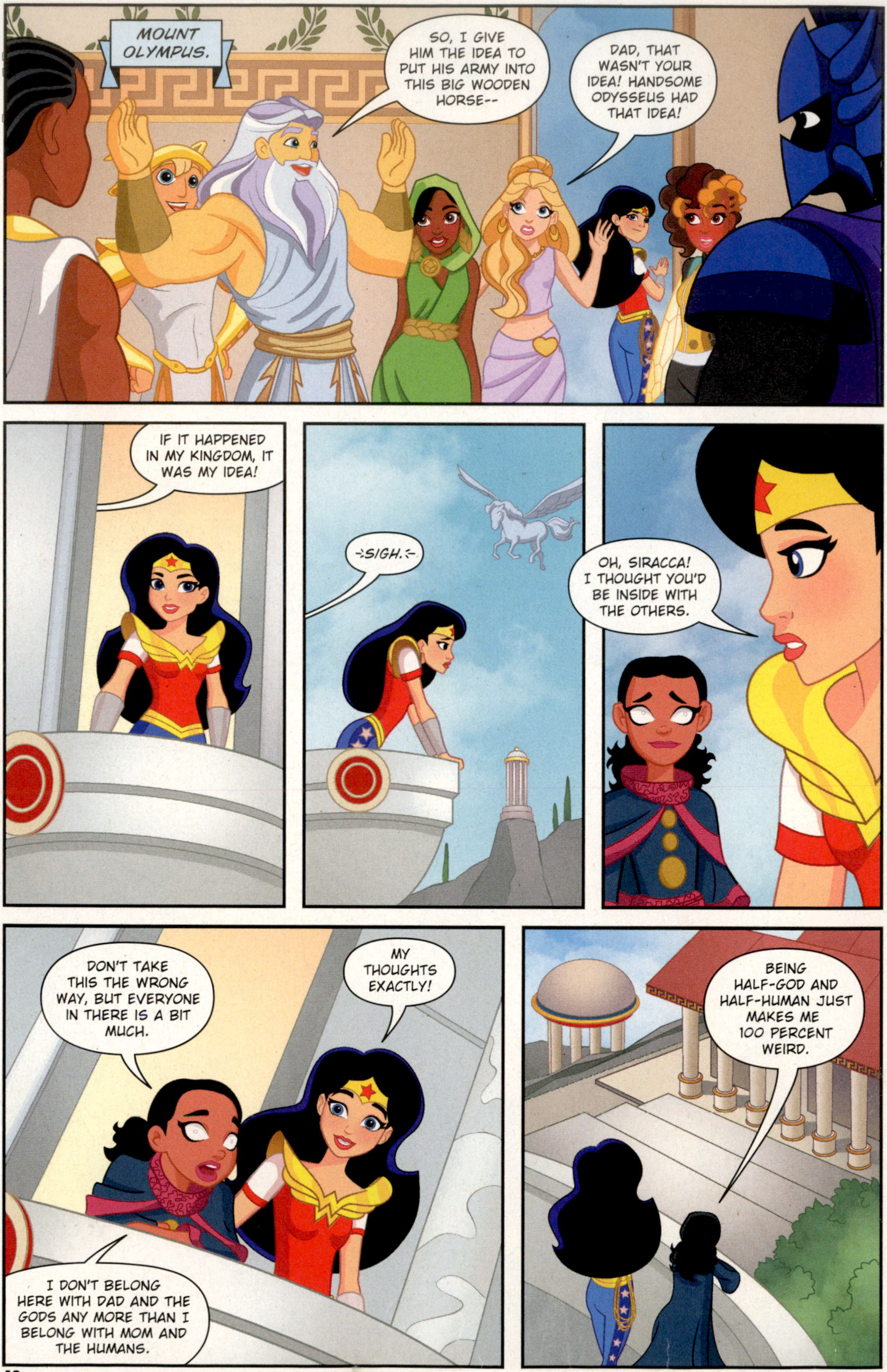
MOUNT OLYMPUS.
SO, I GIVE HIM THE IDEA TO PUT HIS ARMY INTO THIS BIG WOODEN HORSE--
DAD, THAT WASN'T YOUR IDEA! HANDSOME ODYSSEUS HAD THAT IDEA!
IF IT HAPPENED IN MY KINGDOM, IT WAS MY IDEA!
-SIGH.-
OH, SIRACCA! I THOUGHT YOU'D BE INSIDE WITH THE OTHERS.
DON'T TAKE THIS THE WRONG WAY, BUT EVERYONE IN THERE IS A BIT MUCH.
MY THOUGHTS EXACTLY!
I DON'T BELONG HERE WITH DAD AND THE GODS ANY MORE THAN I BELONG WITH MOM AND THE HUMANS.
BEING HALF-GOD AND HALF-HUMAN JUST MAKES ME 100 PERCENT WEIRD.

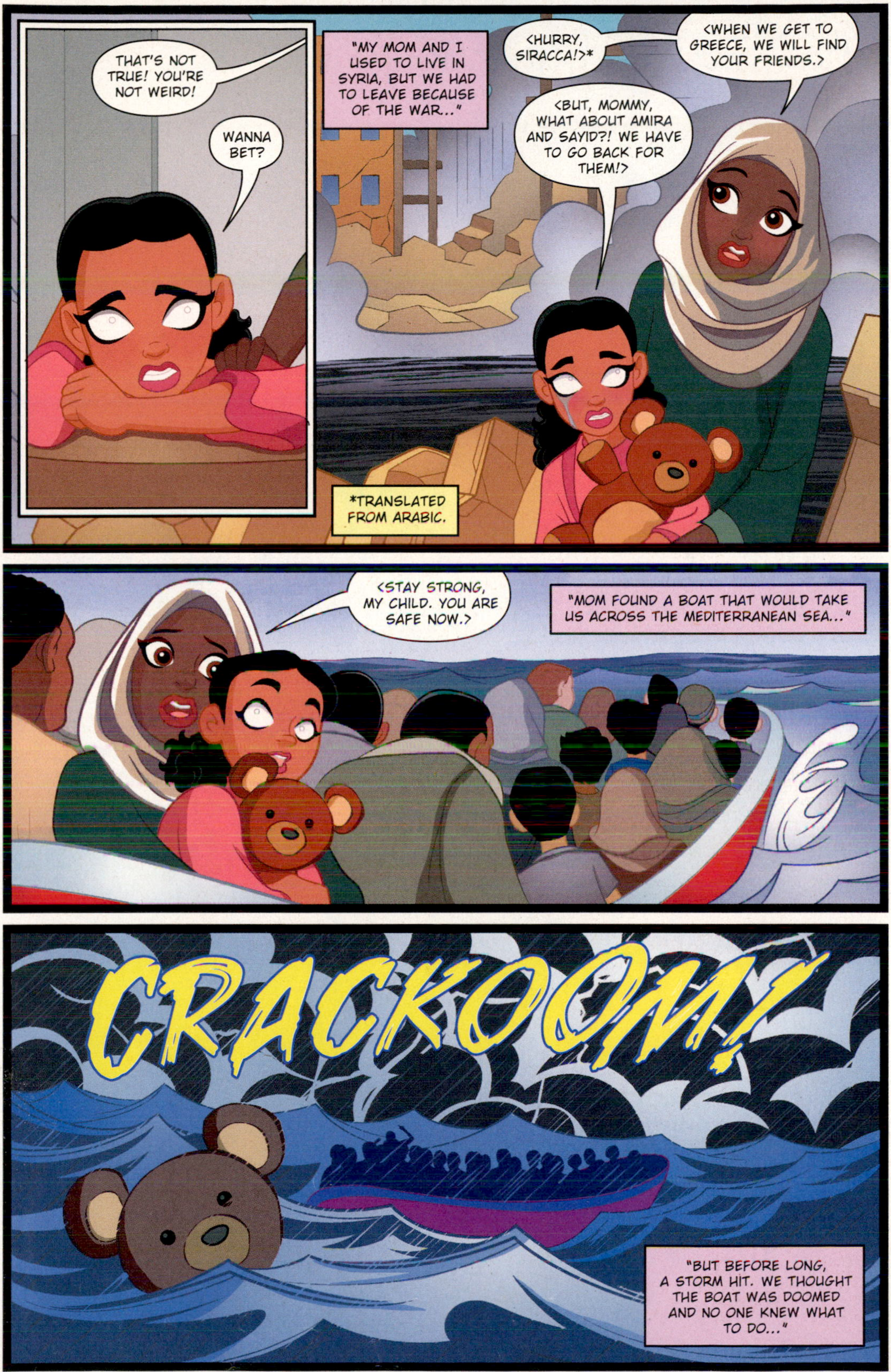
THAT'S NOT TRUE! YOU'RE NOT WEIRD!
WANNA BET?
"MY MOM AND I USED TO LIVE IN SYRIA, BUT WE HAD TO LEAVE BECAUSE OF THE WAR..."
<HURRY, SIRACCA!>*
<WHEN WE GET TO GREECE, WE WILL FIND YOUR FRIENDS.>
<BUT, MOMMY, WHAT ABOUT AMIRA AND SAYID?! WE HAVE TO GO BACK FOR THEM!>
*TRANSLATED FROM ARABIC.
<STAY STRONG, MY CHILD. YOU ARE SAFE NOW.>
"MOM FOUND A BOAT THAT WOULD TAKE US ACROSS THE MEDITERRANEAN SEA..."
CRACKOOM!
"BUT BEFORE LONG, A STORM HIT. WE THOUGHT THE BOAT WAS DOOMED AND NO ONE KNEW WHAT TO DO..."

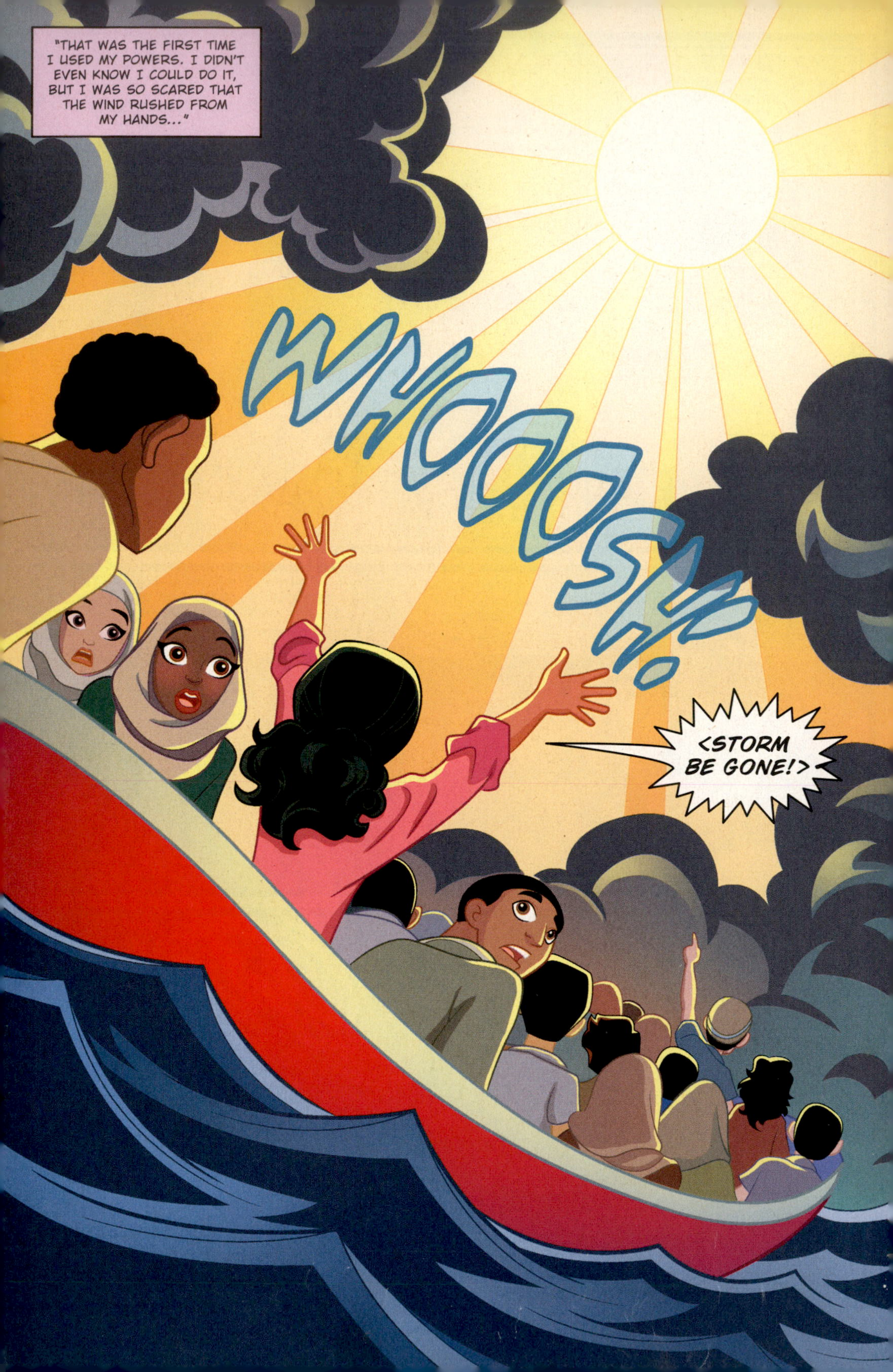
"THAT WAS THE FIRST TIME I USED MY POWERS. I DIDN'T EVEN KNOW I COULD DO IT, BUT I WAS SO SCARED THAT THE WIND RUSHED FROM MY HANDS..."
WHOOOSH!!
<STORM BE GONE!>

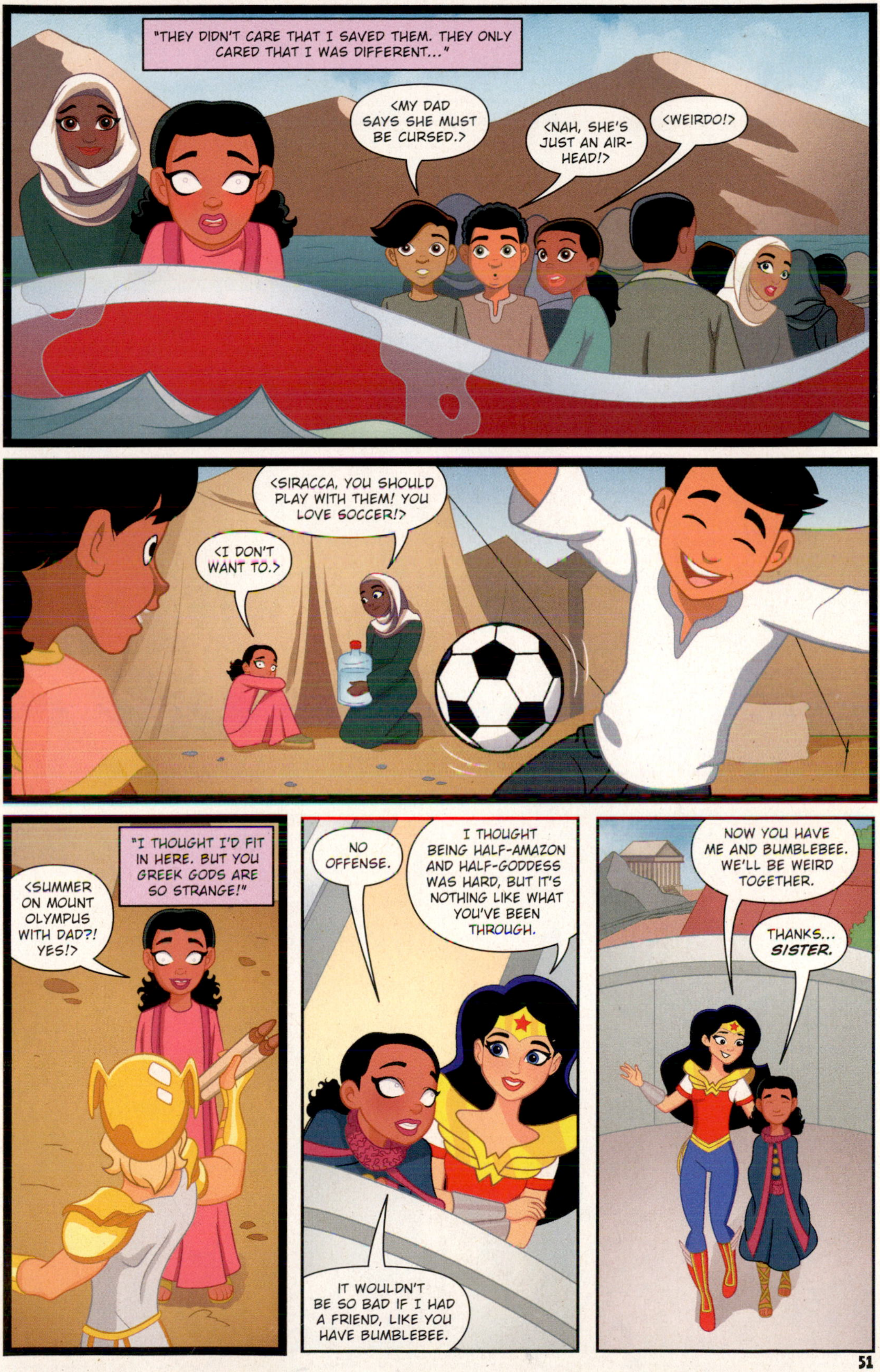
"THEY DIDN'T CARE THAT I SAVED THEM. THEY ONLY CARED THAT I WAS DIFFERENT..."
<MY DAD SAYS SHE MUST BE CURSED.>
<NAH, SHE'S JUST AN AIR-HEAD!>
<WEIRDO!>
<SIRACCA, YOU SHOULD PLAY WITH THEM! YOU LOVE SOCCER!>
<I DON'T WANT TO.>
"I THOUGHT I'D FIT IN HERE. BUT YOU GREEK GODS ARE SO STRANGE!"
<SUMMER ON MOUNT OLYMPUS WITH DAD?! YES!>
NO OFFENSE.
I THOUGHT BEING HALF-AMAZON AND HALF-GODDESS WAS HARD, BUT IT'S NOTHING LIKE WHAT YOU'VE BEEN THROUGH.
IT WOULDN'T BE SO BAD IF I HAD A FRIEND, LIKE YOU HAVE BUMBLEBEE.
NOW YOU HAVE ME AND BUMBLEBEE. WE'LL BE WEIRD TOGETHER.
THANKS... *SISTER.*

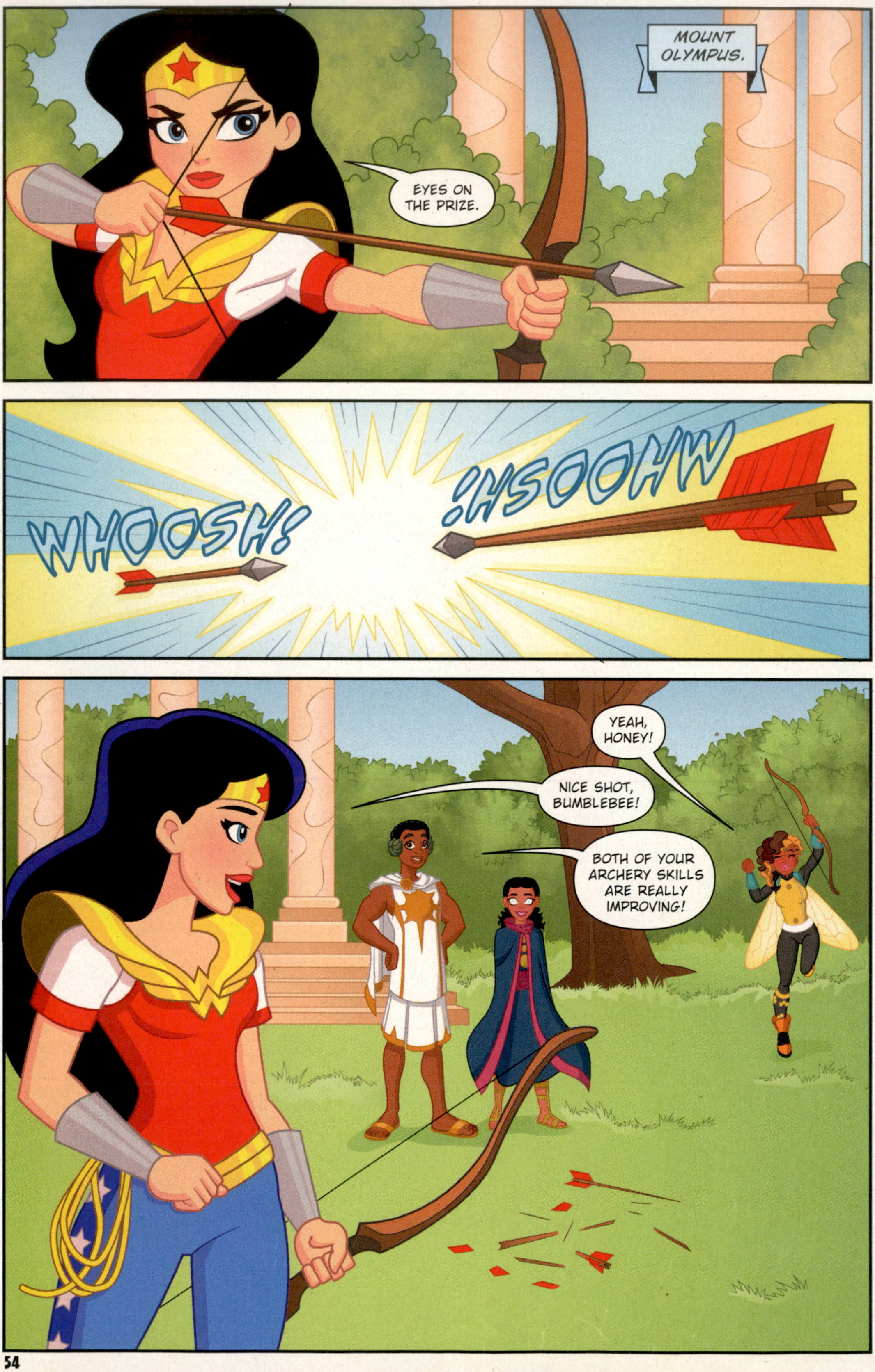
MOUNT OLYMPUS.
EYES ON THE PRIZE.
WHOOSH!
WHOOSH!
YEAH, HONEY!
NICE SHOT, BUMBLEBEE!
BOTH OF YOUR ARCHERY SKILLS ARE REALLY IMPROVING!

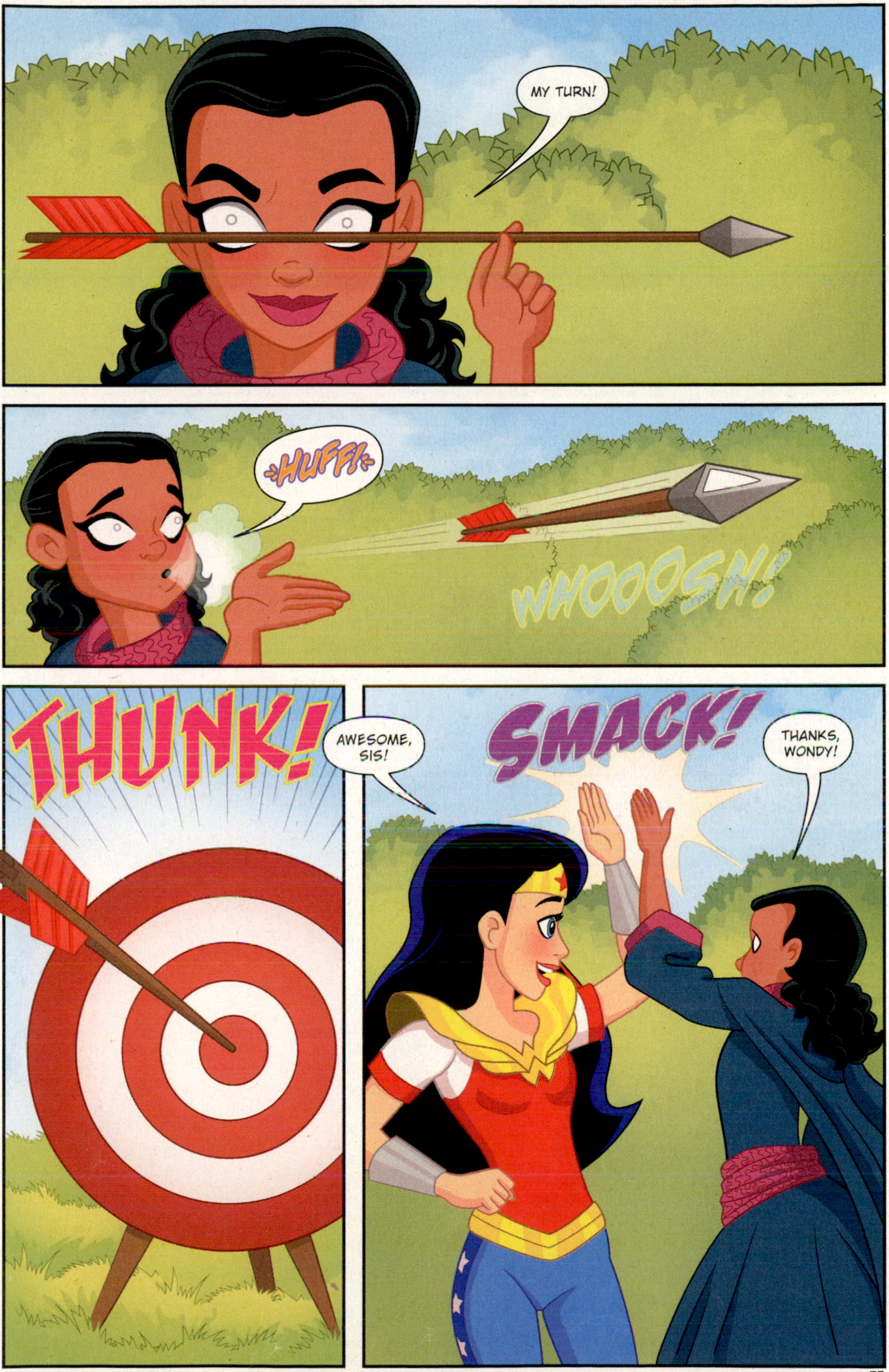
MY TURN!
HUFF!
WHOOOSH!
THUNK!
AWESOME, SIS!
SMACK!
THANKS, WONDY!

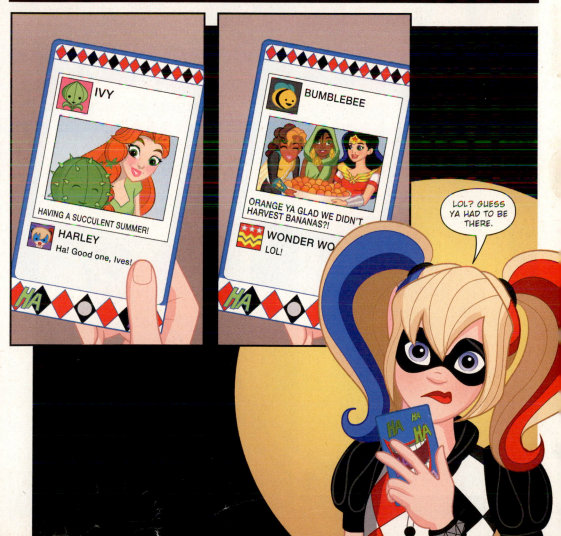

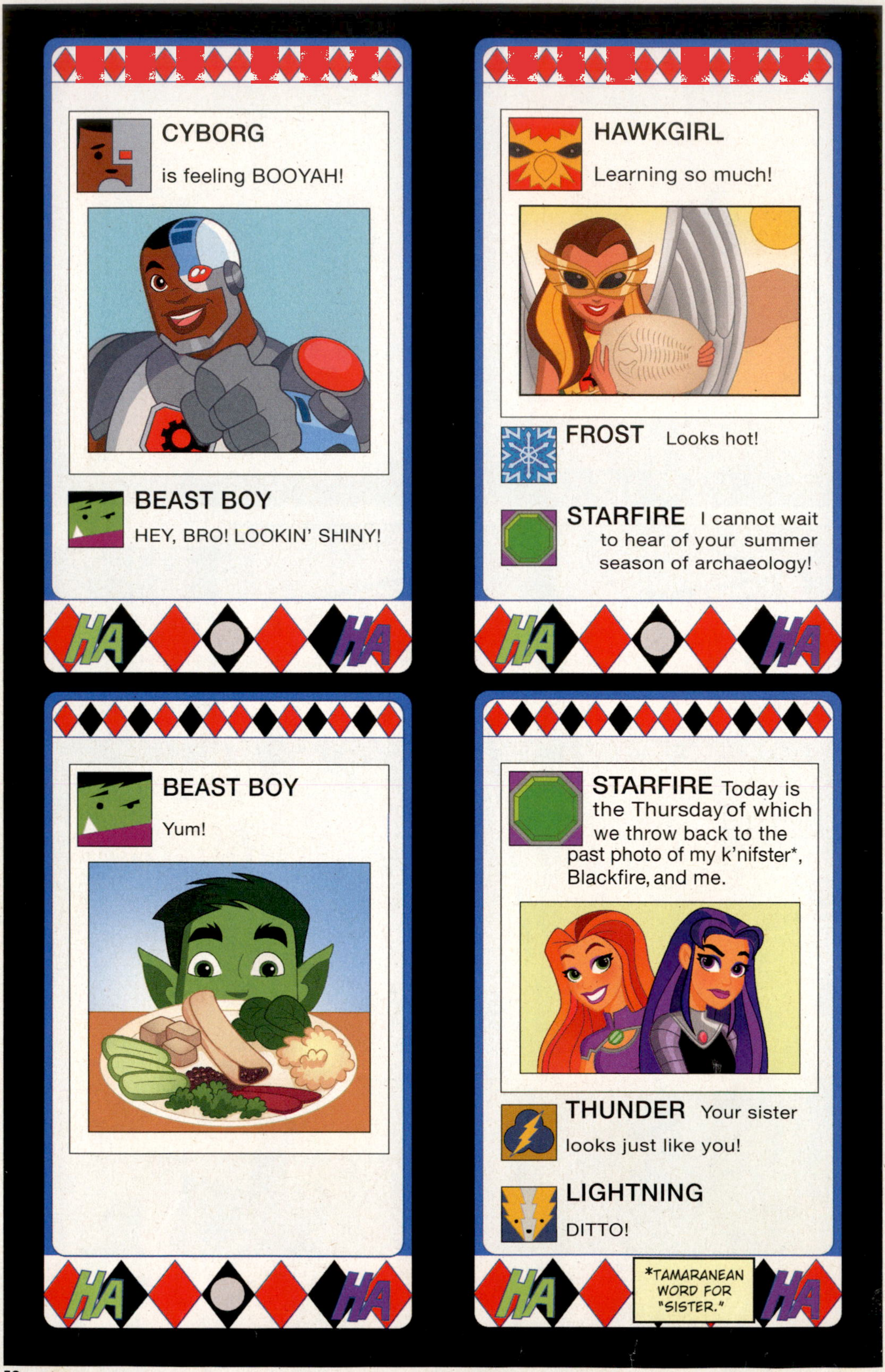
CYBORG
is feeling BOOYAH!
BEAST BOY
HEY, BRO! LOOKIN' SHINY!
HA
HA
HAWKGIRL
Learning so much!
FROST
Looks hot!
STARFIRE
I cannot wait to hear of your summer season of archaeology!
HA
HA
BEAST BOY
Yum!
HA
HA
STARFIRE
Today is the Thursday of which we throw back to the past photo of my k'nifster*, Blackfire, and me.
THUNDER
Your sister looks just like you!
LIGHTNING
DITTO!
HA
*TAMARANEAN WORD FOR "SISTER."
HA

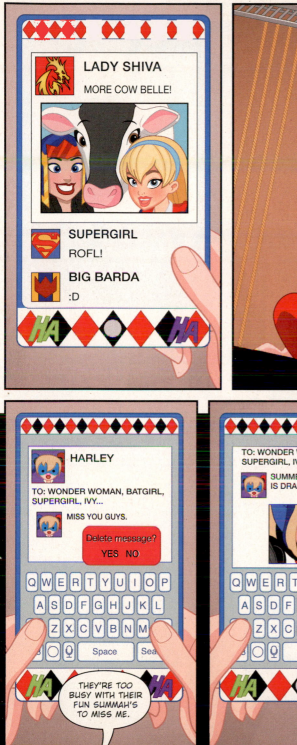

LADY SHIVA
MORE COW BELLE!

SUPERGIRL
ROFL!

BIG BARDA
:D

I HATE BEING ON THE *OUTSIDE* OF ALL THE *INSIDE* JOKES!

HARLEY
TO: WONDER WOMAN, BATGIRL, SUPERGIRL, IVY...
MISS YOU GUYS.

Delete message?
YES   NO

THEY'RE TOO BUSY WITH THEIR FUN SUMMAH'S TO MISS ME.

TO: WONDER WOMAN, BATGIRL, SUPERGIRL, IVY...
SUMMER THEATER CAMP IS DRAMATICALLY FUN!

I CAN'T WAIT TILL SCHOOL STARTS AND I GET MY GAL PALS BACK!

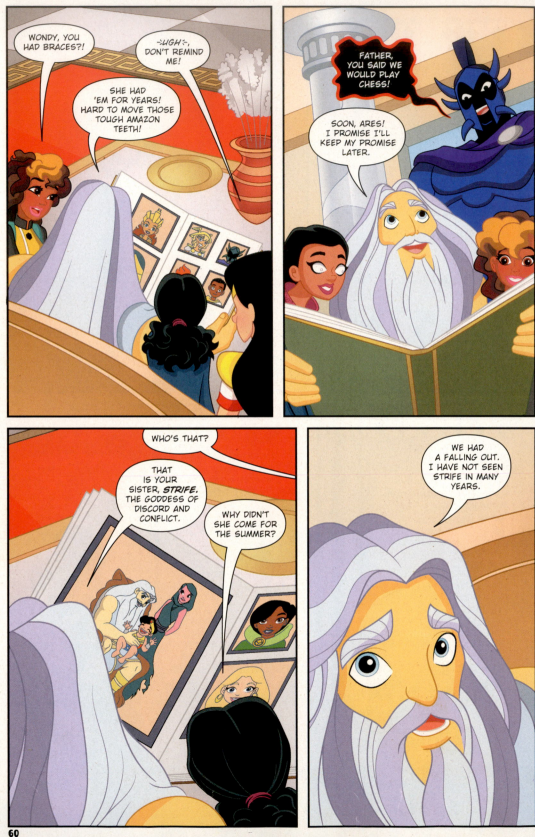

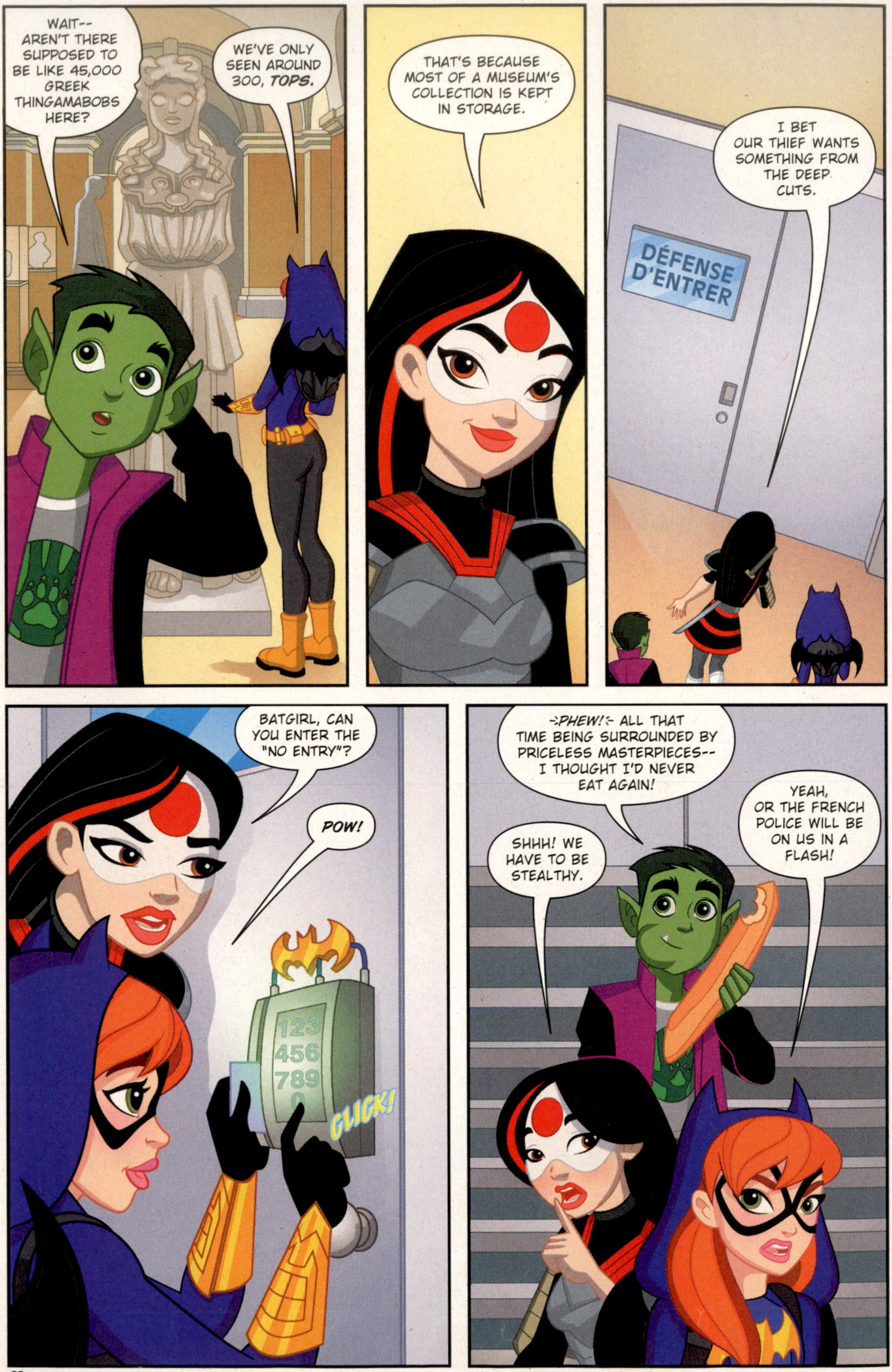
WAIT-- AREN'T THERE SUPPOSED TO BE LIKE 45,000 GREEK THINGAMABOBS HERE?
WE'VE ONLY SEEN AROUND 300, *TOPS.*
THAT'S BECAUSE MOST OF A MUSEUM'S COLLECTION IS KEPT IN STORAGE.
I BET OUR THIEF WANTS SOMETHING FROM THE DEEP CUTS.
DÉFENSE D'ENTRER
BATGIRL, CAN YOU ENTER THE "NO ENTRY"?
POW!
123
456
789
0
CLICK!
PHEW! ALL THAT TIME BEING SURROUNDED BY PRICELESS MASTERPIECES-- I THOUGHT I'D NEVER EAT AGAIN!
SHHH! WE HAVE TO BE STEALTHY.
YEAH, OR THE FRENCH POLICE WILL BE ON US IN A FLASH!

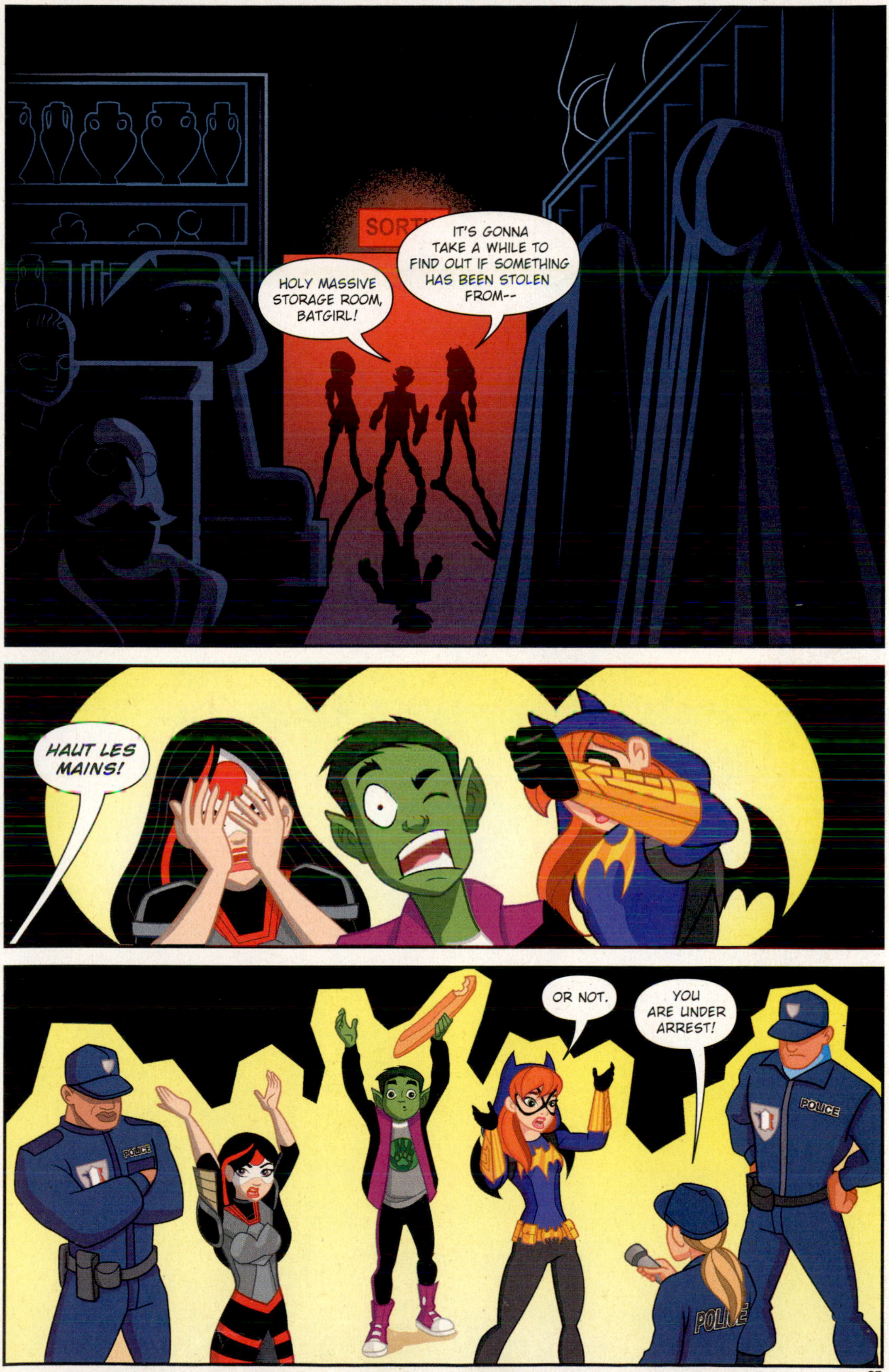
SORTI
HOLY MASSIVE STORAGE ROOM, BATGIRL!
IT'S GONNA TAKE A WHILE TO FIND OUT IF SOMETHING HAS BEEN STOLEN FROM--
HAUT LES MAINS!
OR NOT.
YOU ARE UNDER ARREST!
POLICE
POLICE
POLICE

TO BE CONTINUED...

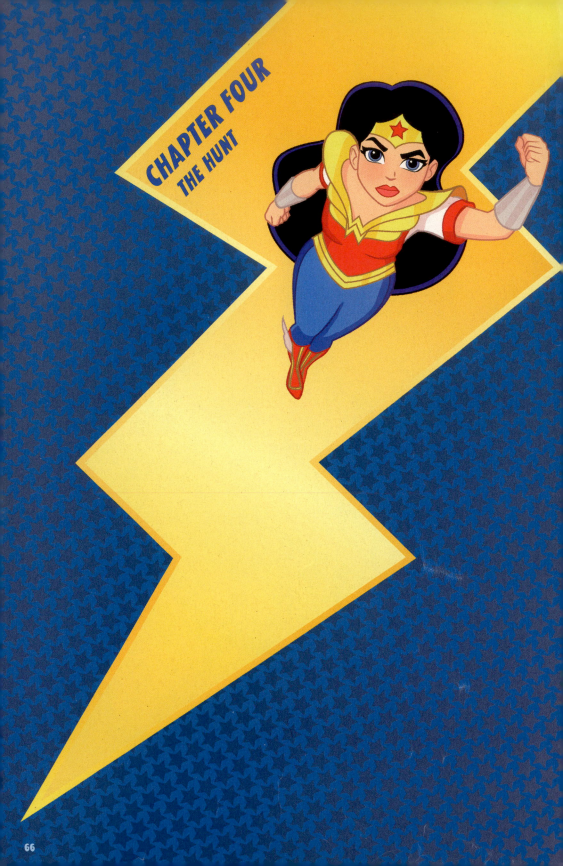

CHAPTER FOUR
THE HUNT

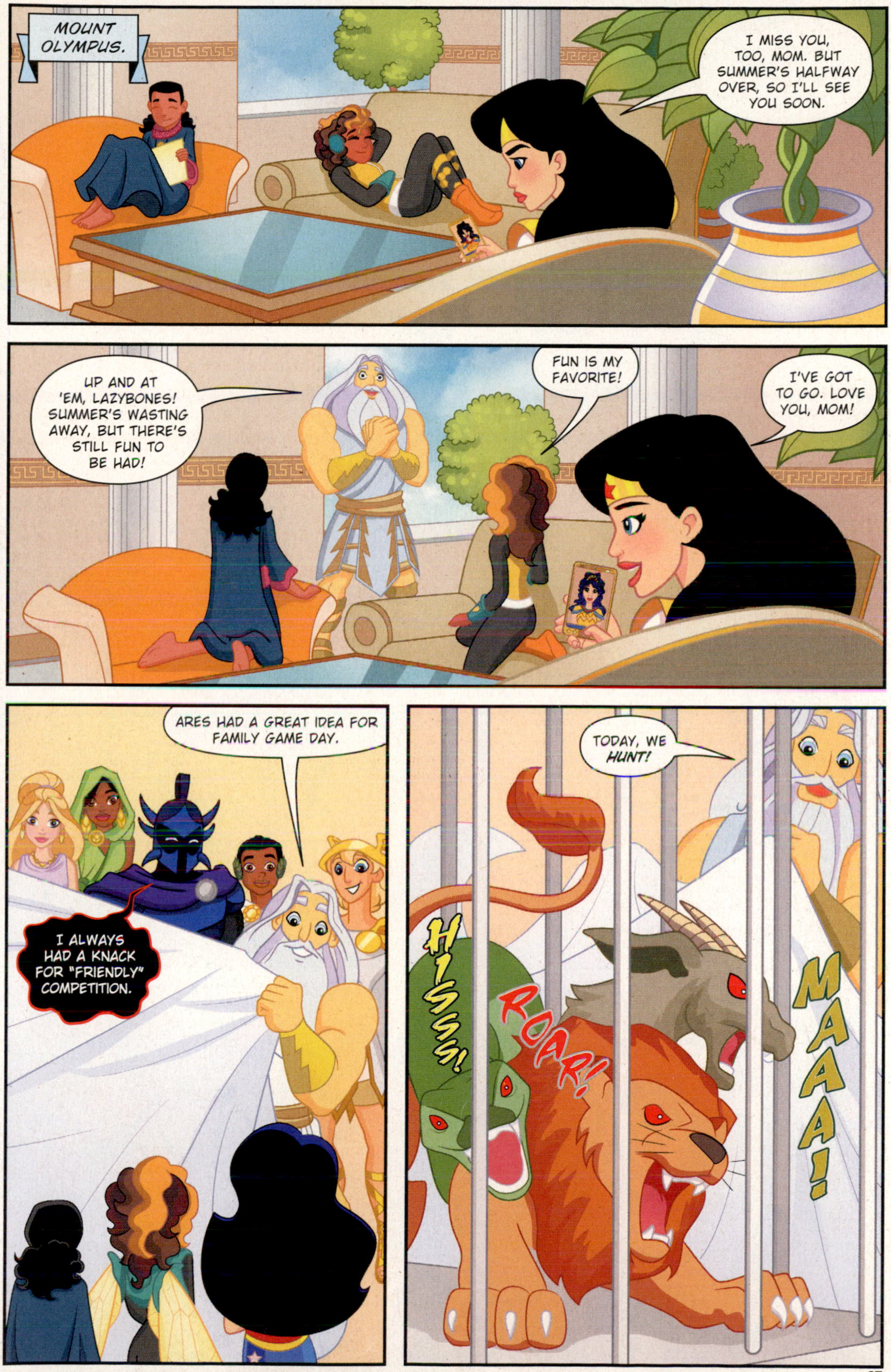

MOUNT OLYMPUS.
I MISS YOU, TOO, MOM. BUT SUMMER'S HALFWAY OVER, SO I'LL SEE YOU SOON.
UP AND AT 'EM, LAZYBONES! SUMMER'S WASTING AWAY, BUT THERE'S STILL FUN TO BE HAD!
FUN IS MY FAVORITE!
I'VE GOT TO GO. LOVE YOU, MOM!
ARES HAD A GREAT IDEA FOR FAMILY GAME DAY.
I ALWAYS HAD A KNACK FOR "FRIENDLY" COMPETITION.
TODAY, WE HUNT!
HISSS!
ROAR!
MAAAA!

71

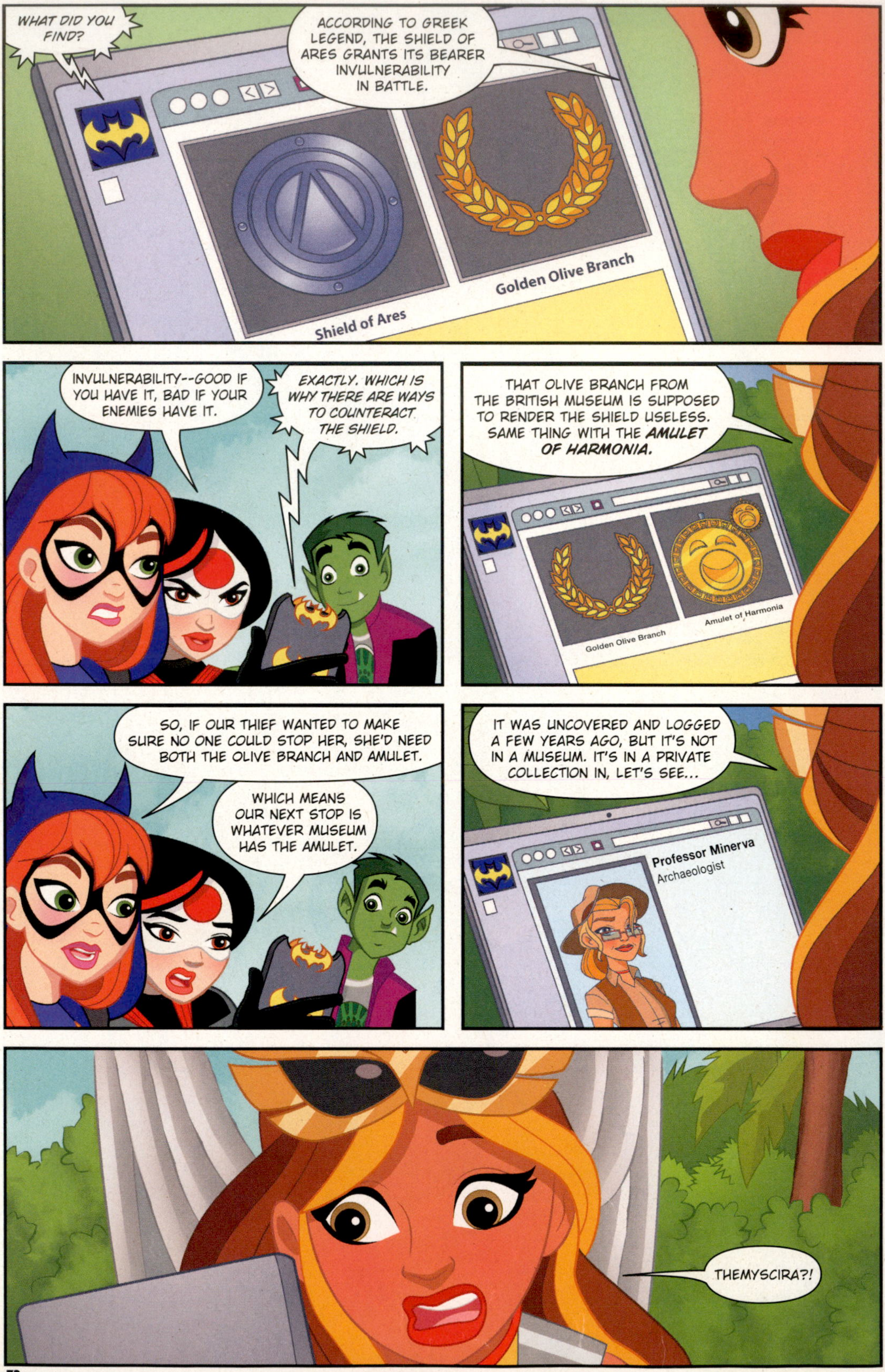
WHAT DID YOU FIND?
ACCORDING TO GREEK LEGEND, THE SHIELD OF ARES GRANTS ITS BEARER INVULNERABILITY IN BATTLE.
Shield of Ares
Golden Olive Branch
INVULNERABILITY--GOOD IF YOU HAVE IT, BAD IF YOUR ENEMIES HAVE IT.
EXACTLY. WHICH IS WHY THERE ARE WAYS TO COUNTERACT THE SHIELD.
THAT OLIVE BRANCH FROM THE BRITISH MUSEUM IS SUPPOSED TO RENDER THE SHIELD USELESS. SAME THING WITH THE AMULET OF HARMONIA.
Golden Olive Branch
Amulet of Harmonia
SO, IF OUR THIEF WANTED TO MAKE SURE NO ONE COULD STOP HER, SHE'D NEED BOTH THE OLIVE BRANCH AND AMULET.
WHICH MEANS OUR NEXT STOP IS WHATEVER MUSEUM HAS THE AMULET.
IT WAS UNCOVERED AND LOGGED A FEW YEARS AGO, BUT IT'S NOT IN A MUSEUM. IT'S IN A PRIVATE COLLECTION IN, LET'S SEE...
Professor Minerva
Archaeologist
THEMYSCIRA?!

73

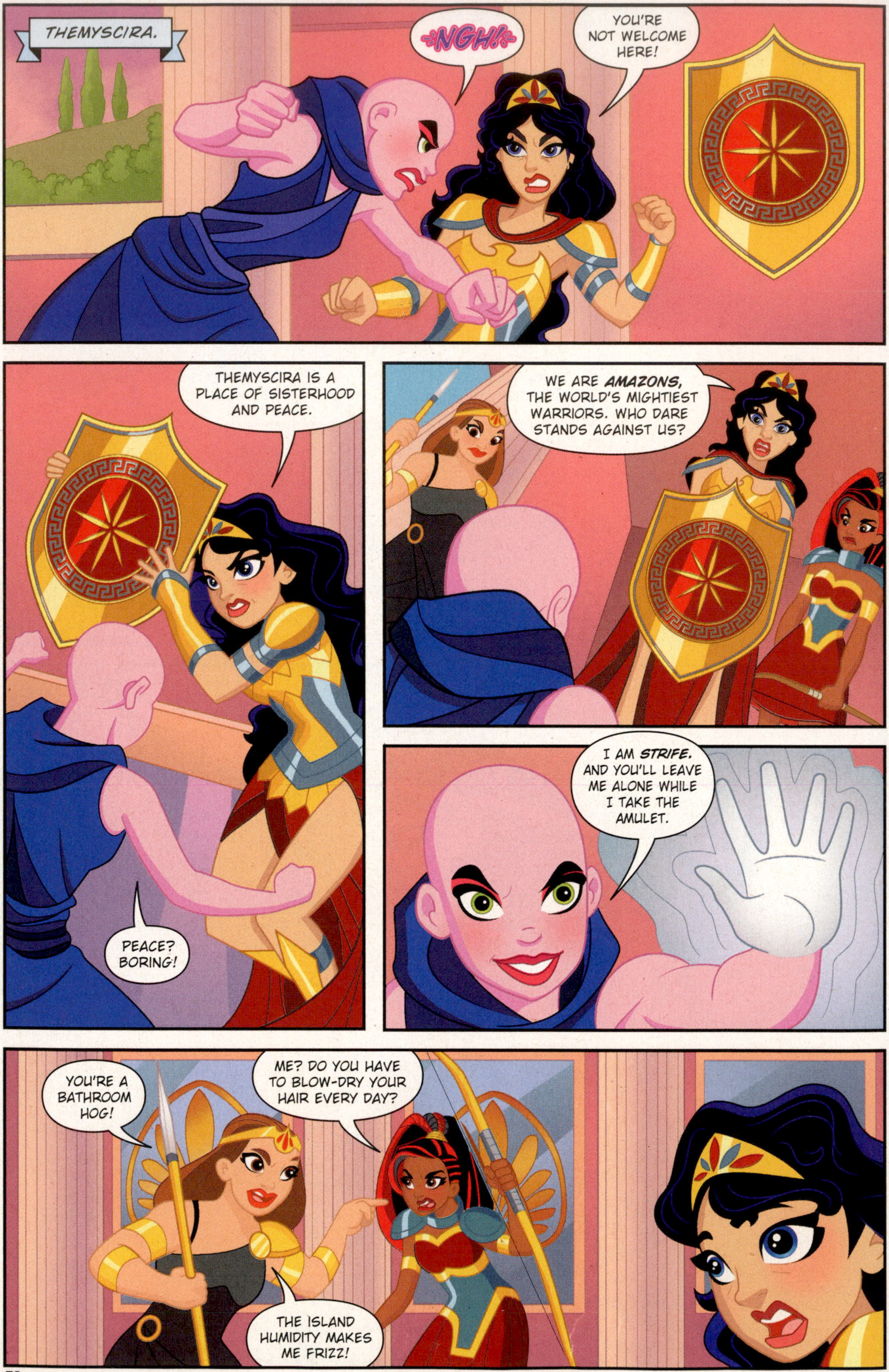
THEMYSCIRA.
NGH!
YOU'RE NOT WELCOME HERE!
THEMYSCIRA IS A PLACE OF SISTERHOOD AND PEACE.
PEACE? BORING!
WE ARE AMAZONS, THE WORLD'S MIGHTIEST WARRIORS. WHO DARE STANDS AGAINST US?
I AM STRIFE. AND YOU'LL LEAVE ME ALONE WHILE I TAKE THE AMULET.
YOU'RE A BATHROOM HOG!
ME? DO YOU HAVE TO BLOW-DRY YOUR HAIR EVERY DAY?
THE ISLAND HUMIDITY MAKES ME FRIZZ!

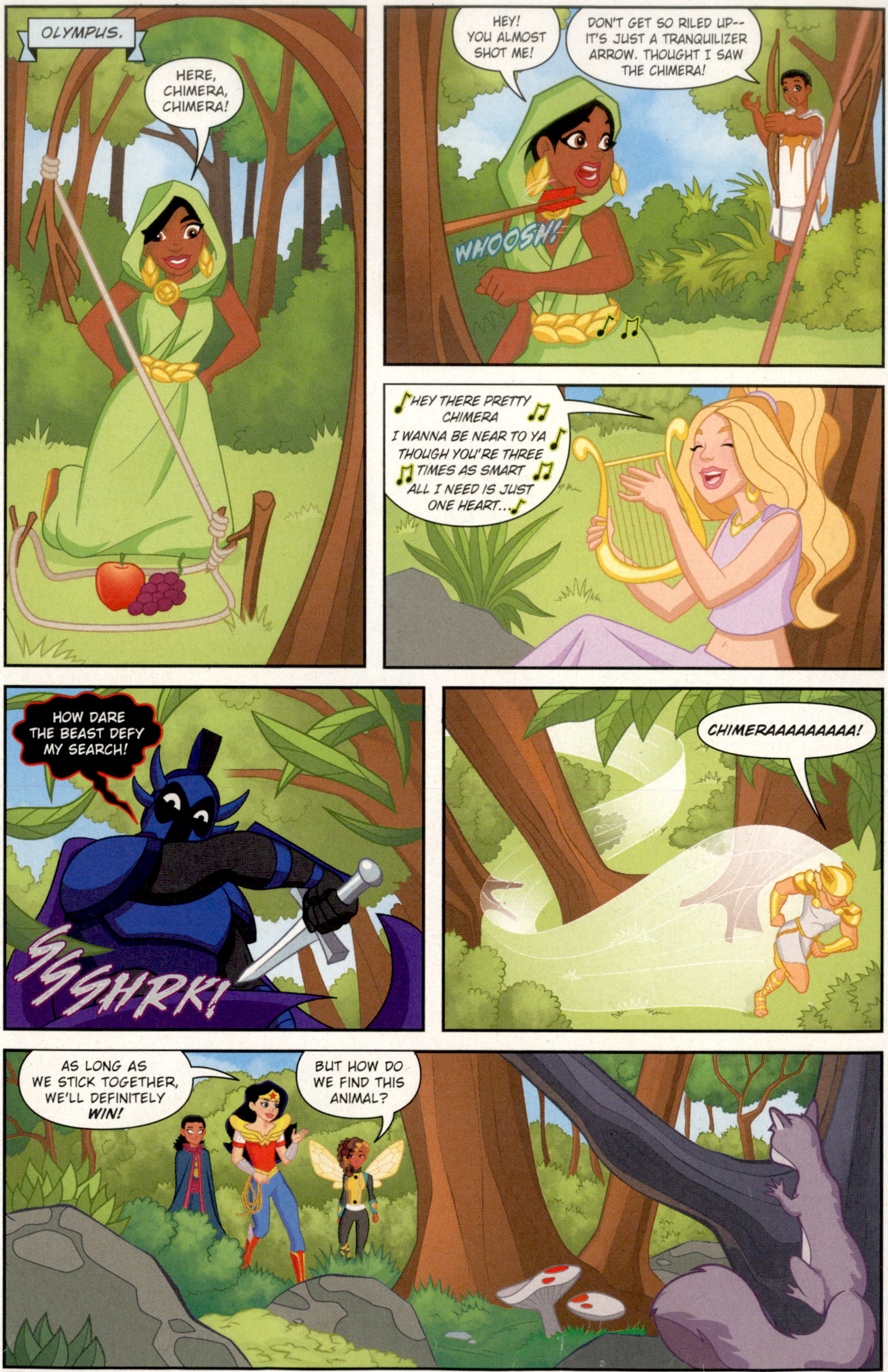
OLYMPUS.
HERE, CHIMERA, CHIMERA!
HEY! YOU ALMOST SHOT ME!
DON'T GET SO RILED UP-- IT'S JUST A TRANQUILIZER ARROW. THOUGHT I SAW THE CHIMERA!
WHOOSH!
HEY THERE PRETTY CHIMERA I WANNA BE NEAR TO YA THOUGH YOU'RE THREE TIMES AS SMART ALL I NEED IS JUST ONE HEART...
HOW DARE THE BEAST DEFY MY SEARCH!
SSSHRK!
CHIMERAAAAAAAAAA!
AS LONG AS WE STICK TOGETHER, WE'LL DEFINITELY WIN!
BUT HOW DO WE FIND THIS ANIMAL?

THE WIND WILL TELL US WHERE THE CHIMERA IS.

WWHHHHSSSSSHHHH

"IT BLOWS ACROSS THE MOUNTAIN, SEARCHING EVERY BRANCH AND BURROW."

WWWHHHHSSSSSHHHH

THIS WAY!

NICE SUPERPOWERS, SIRACCA!

ALL RIGHT, *BEASTY BUDDY*, YOU'RE COMING HOME WITH US.

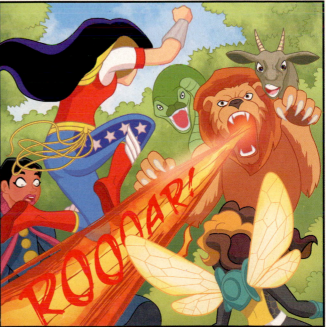

ROOOAR!

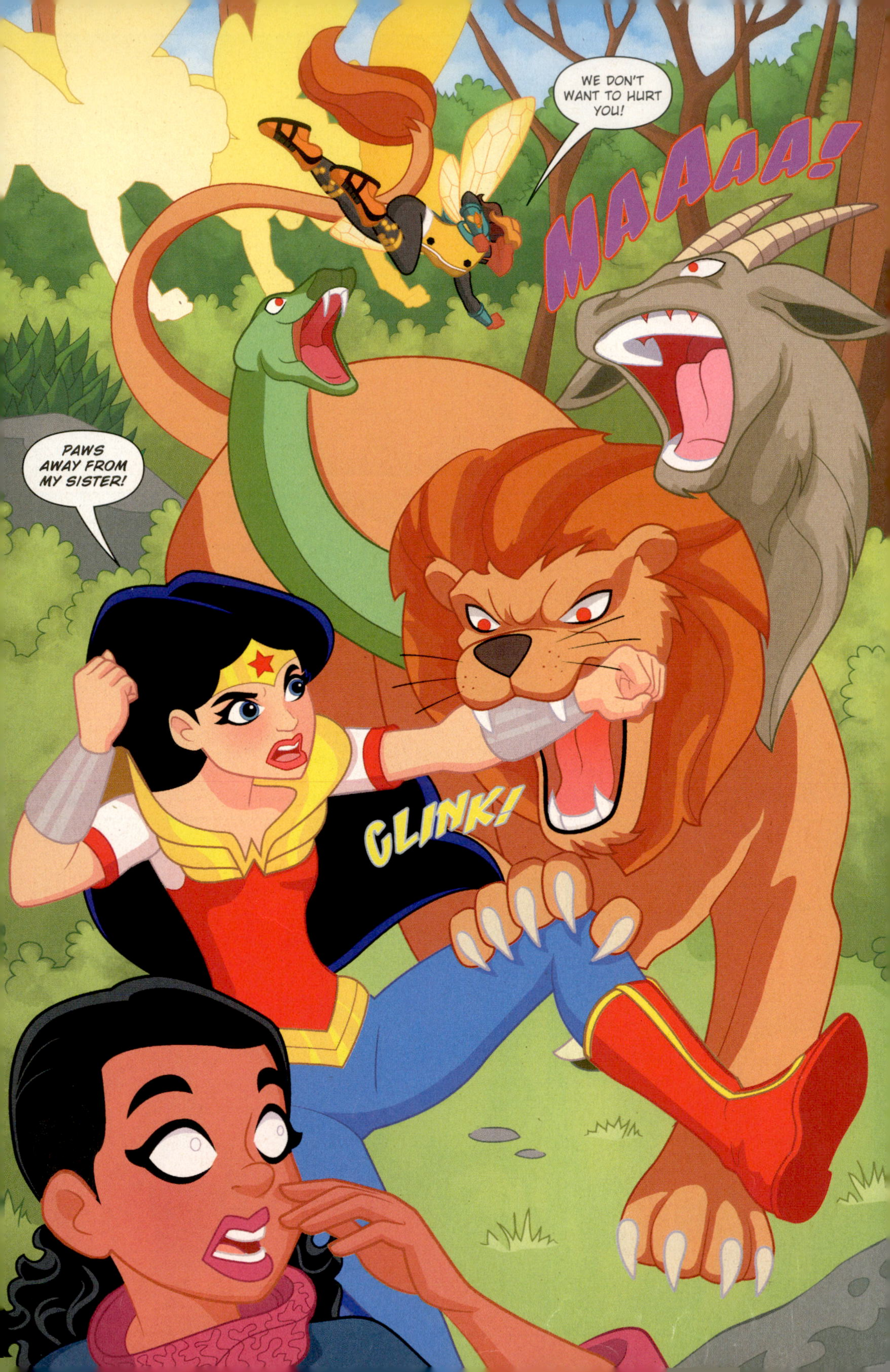
WE DON'T WANT TO HURT YOU!
MAAAA!
PAWS AWAY FROM MY SISTER!
CLINK!

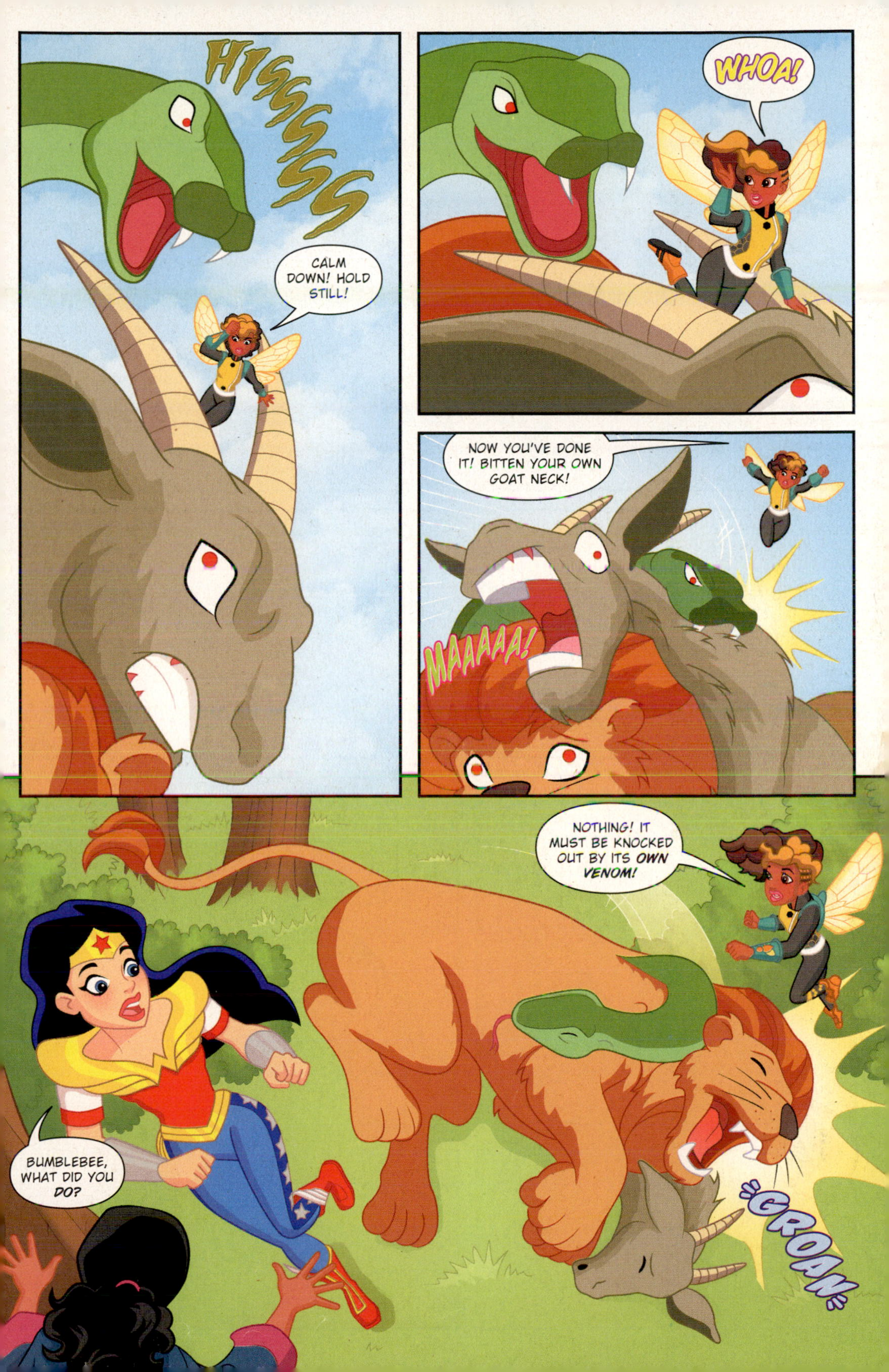
HISSSSS
CALM DOWN! HOLD STILL!
WHOA!
NOW YOU'VE DONE IT! BITTEN YOUR OWN GOAT NECK!
MAAAAA!
NOTHING! IT MUST BE KNOCKED OUT BY ITS OWN VENOM!
BUMBLEBEE, WHAT DID YOU DO?
GROAN

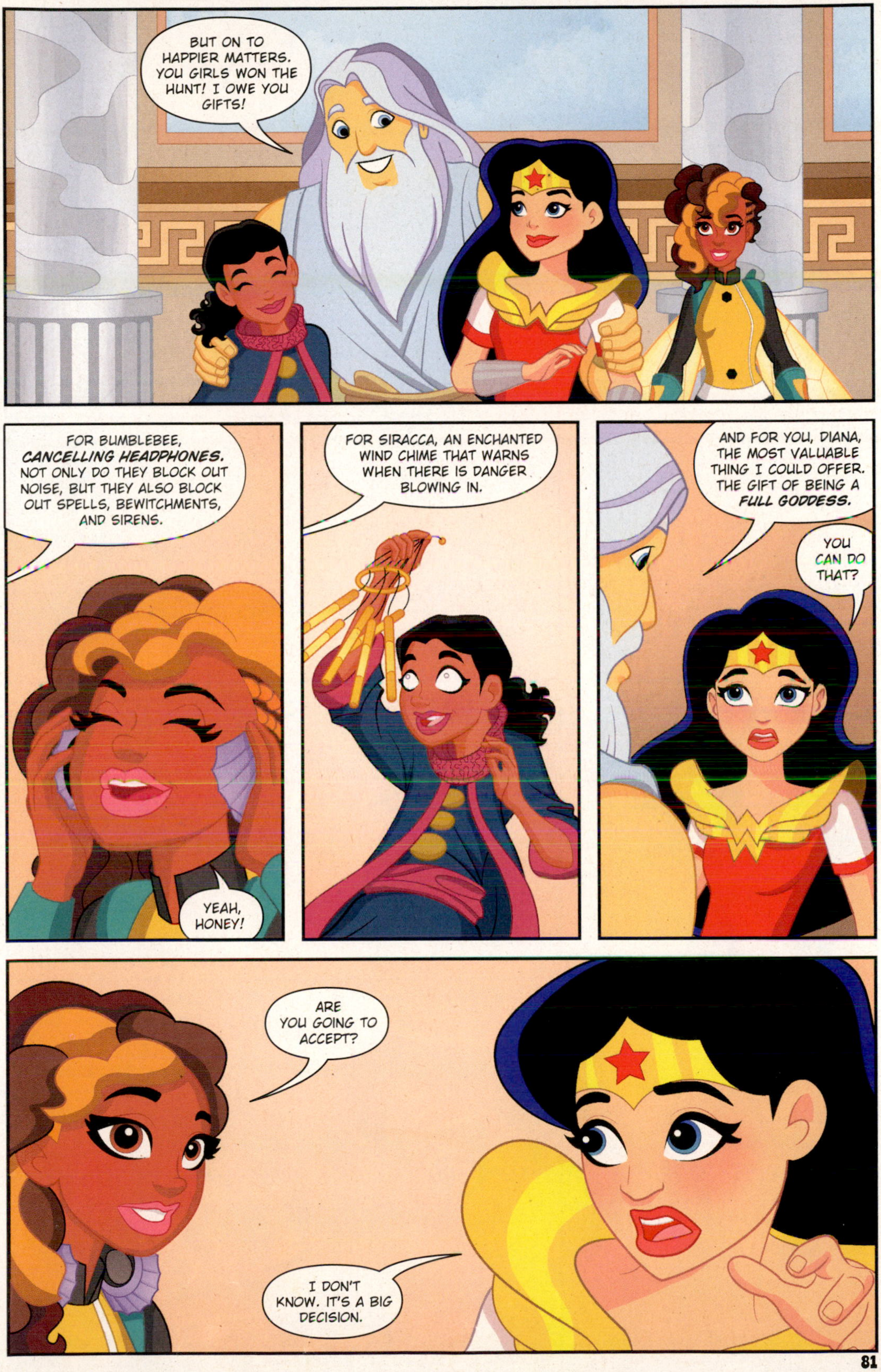
BUT ON TO HAPPIER MATTERS. YOU GIRLS WON THE HUNT! I OWE YOU GIFTS!
FOR BUMBLEBEE, *CANCELLING HEADPHONES.* NOT ONLY DO THEY BLOCK OUT NOISE, BUT THEY ALSO BLOCK OUT SPELLS, BEWITCHMENTS, AND SIRENS.
YEAH, HONEY!
FOR SIRACCA, AN ENCHANTED WIND CHIME THAT WARNS WHEN THERE IS DANGER BLOWING IN.
AND FOR YOU, DIANA, THE MOST VALUABLE THING I COULD OFFER. THE GIFT OF BEING A *FULL GODDESS.*
YOU CAN DO THAT?
ARE YOU GOING TO ACCEPT?
I DON'T KNOW. IT'S A BIG DECISION.

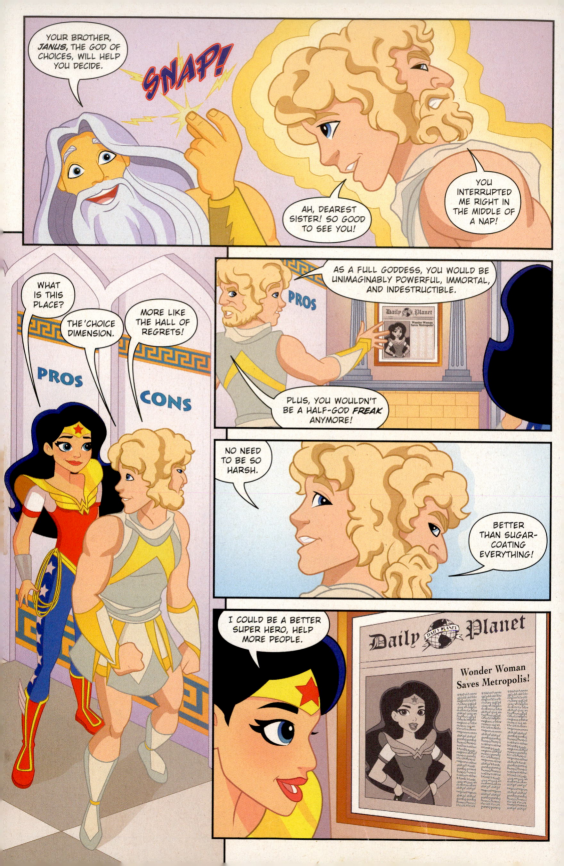

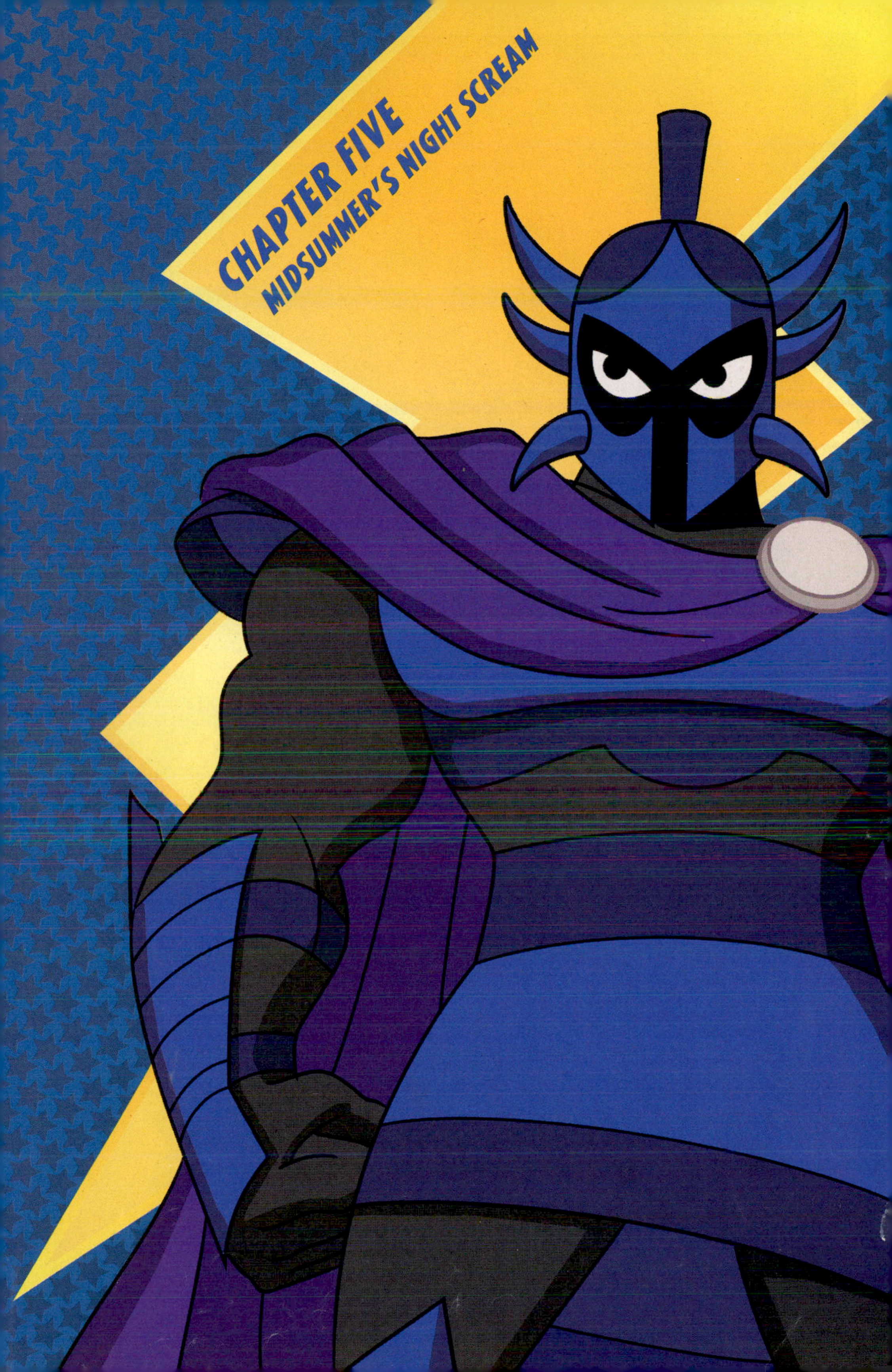
CHAPTER FIVE
MIDSUMMER'S NIGHT SCREAM

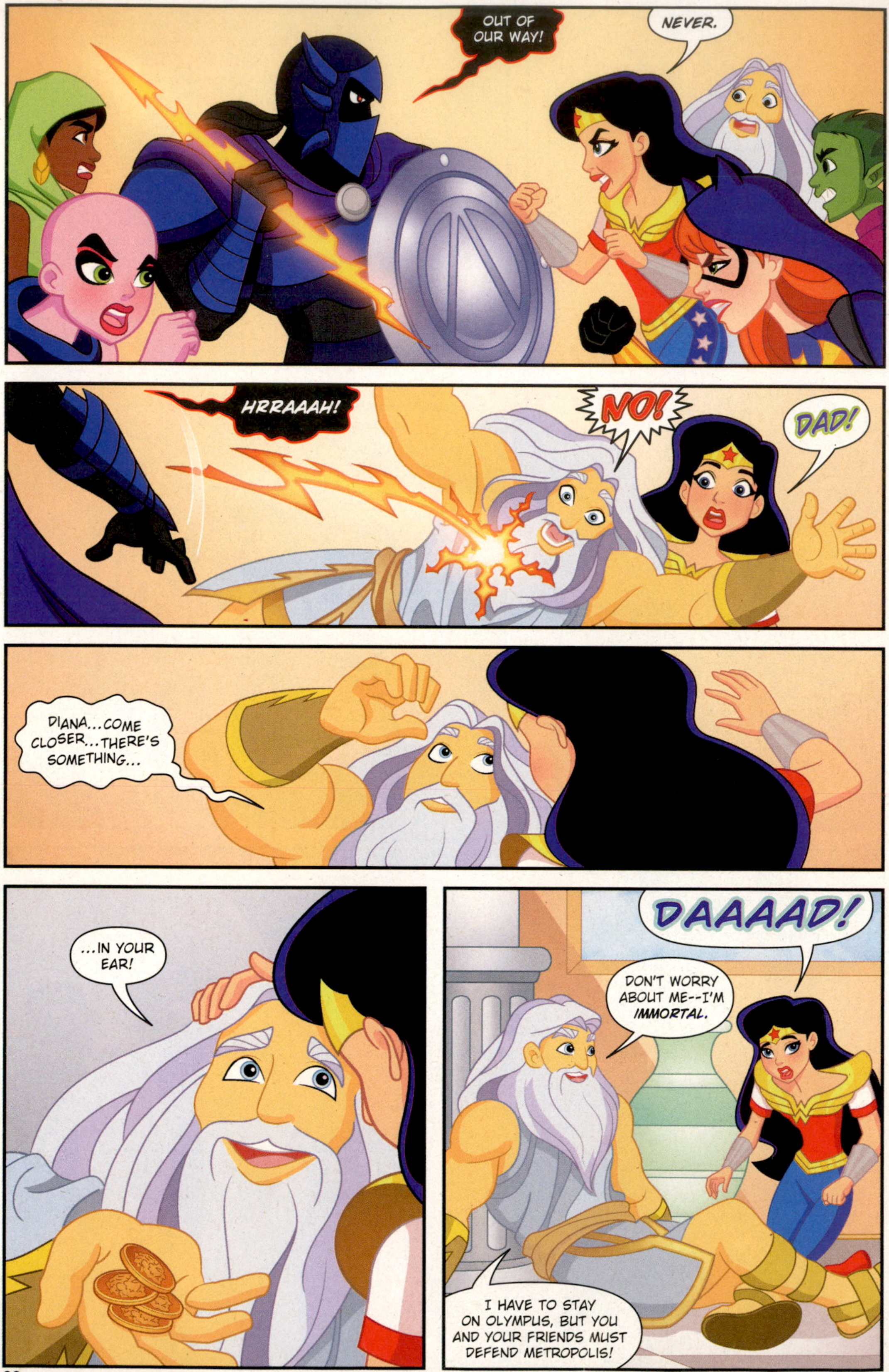
OUT OF OUR WAY!
NEVER.
HRRAAAH!
NO!
DAD!
DIANA...COME CLOSER...THERE'S SOMETHING...
...IN YOUR EAR!
DAAAAD!
DON'T WORRY ABOUT ME--I'M IMMORTAL.
I HAVE TO STAY ON OLYMPUS, BUT YOU AND YOUR FRIENDS MUST DEFEND METROPOLIS!

89

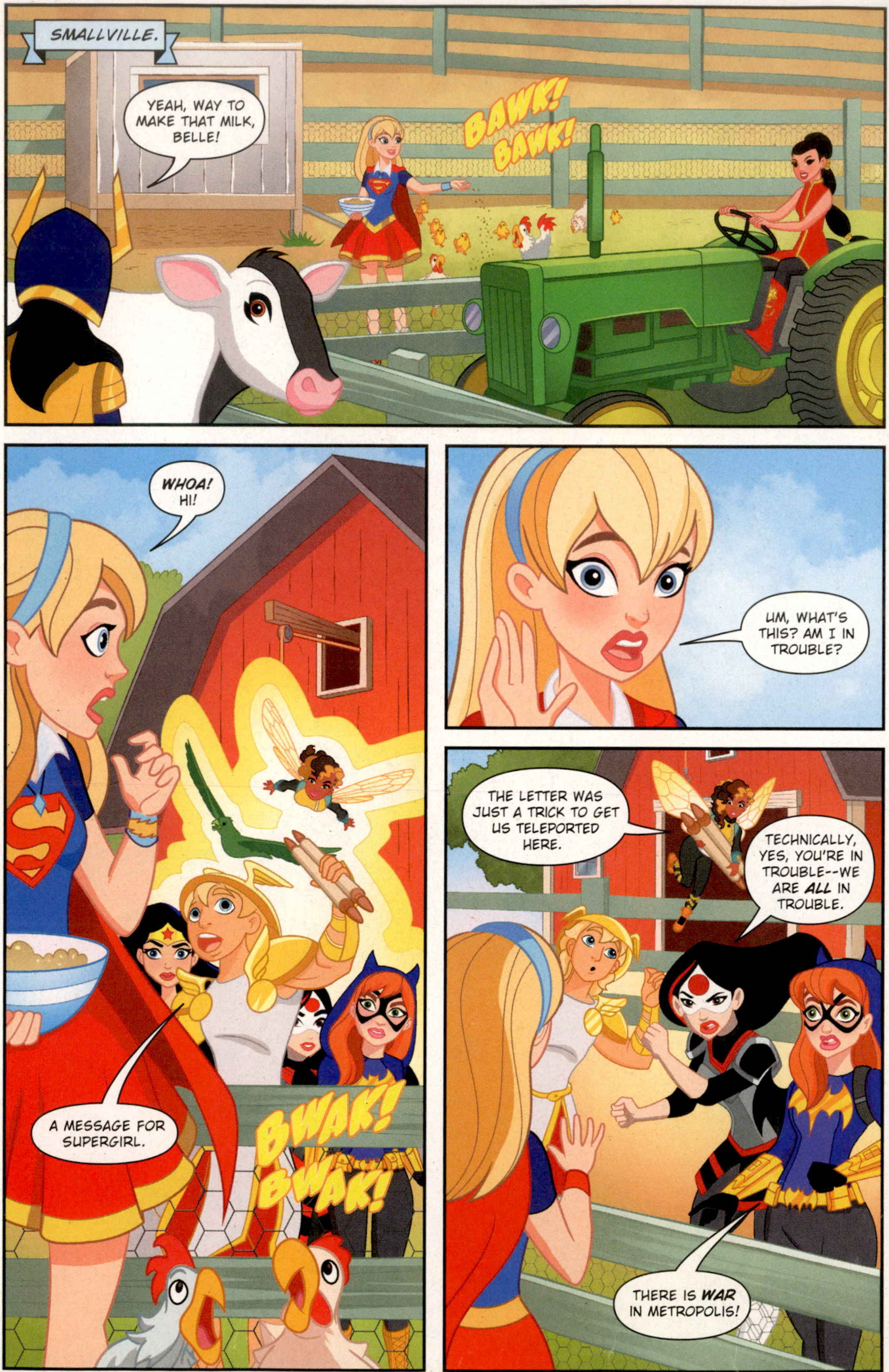
SMALLVILLE.
YEAH, WAY TO MAKE THAT MILK, BELLE!
BAWK! BAWK!
WHOA! HI!
A MESSAGE FOR SUPERGIRL.
BWAK! BWAK!
UM, WHAT'S THIS? AM I IN TROUBLE?
THE LETTER WAS JUST A TRICK TO GET US TELEPORTED HERE.
TECHNICALLY, YES, YOU'RE IN TROUBLE--WE ARE ALL IN TROUBLE.
THERE IS WAR IN METROPOLIS!

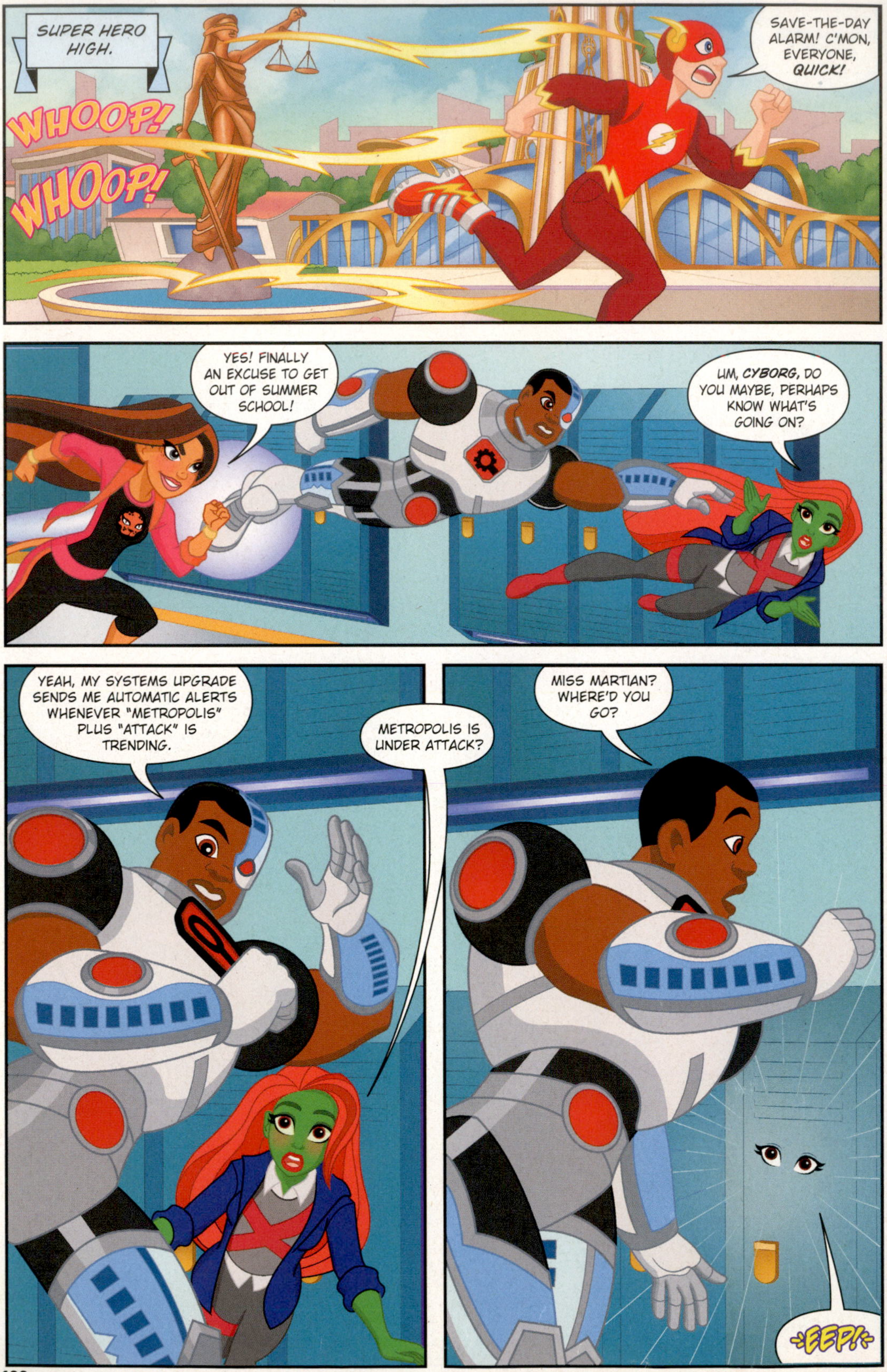
SUPER HERO HIGH.
WHOOP! WHOOP!
SAVE-THE-DAY ALARM! C'MON, EVERYONE, QUICK!
YES! FINALLY AN EXCUSE TO GET OUT OF SUMMER SCHOOL!
UM, CYBORG, DO YOU MAYBE, PERHAPS KNOW WHAT'S GOING ON?
YEAH, MY SYSTEMS UPGRADE SENDS ME AUTOMATIC ALERTS WHENEVER "METROPOLIS" PLUS "ATTACK" IS TRENDING.
METROPOLIS IS UNDER ATTACK?
MISS MARTIAN? WHERE'D YOU GO?
EEP!

CHAPTER SIX
BACK TO SCHOOL

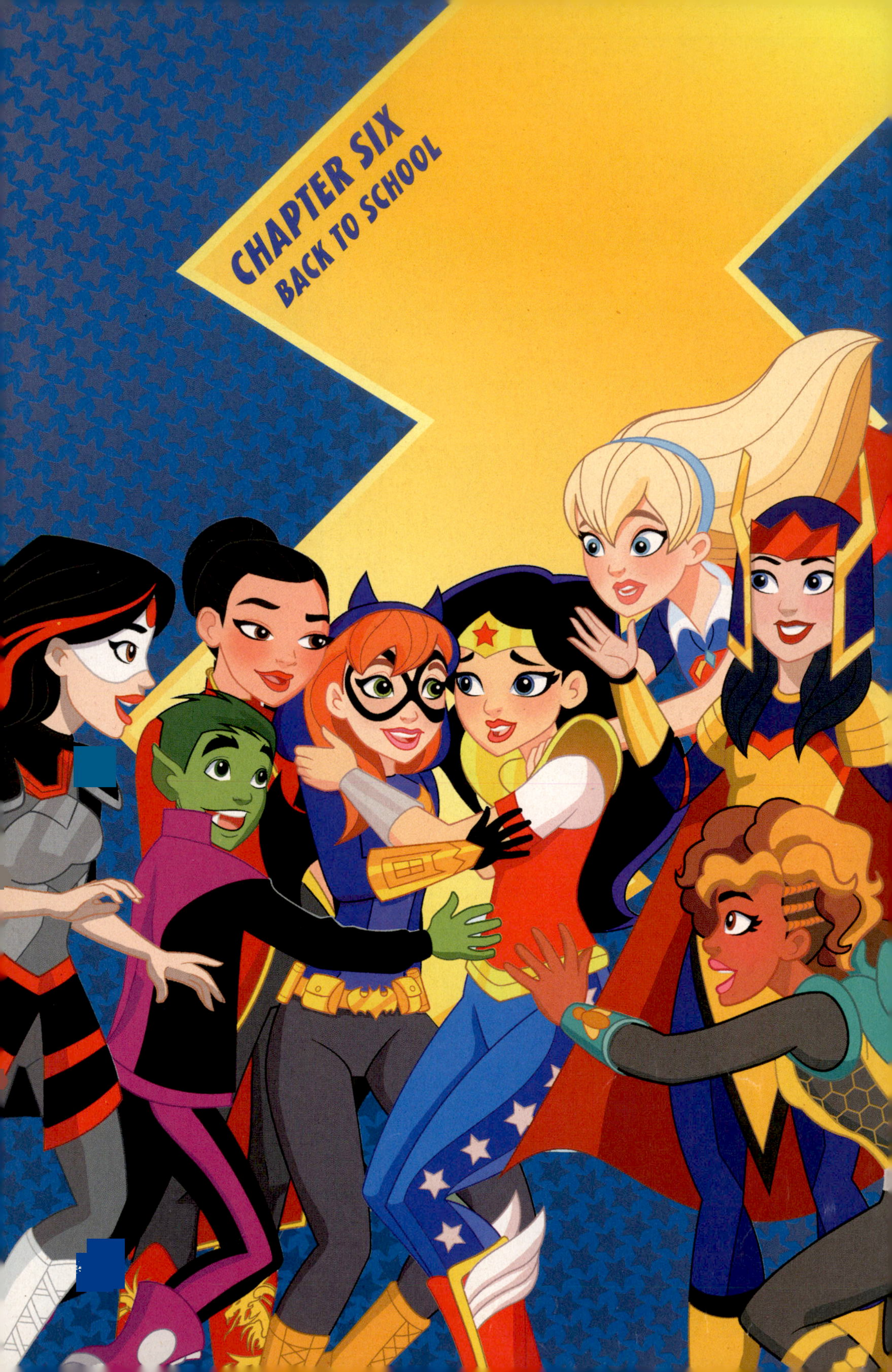

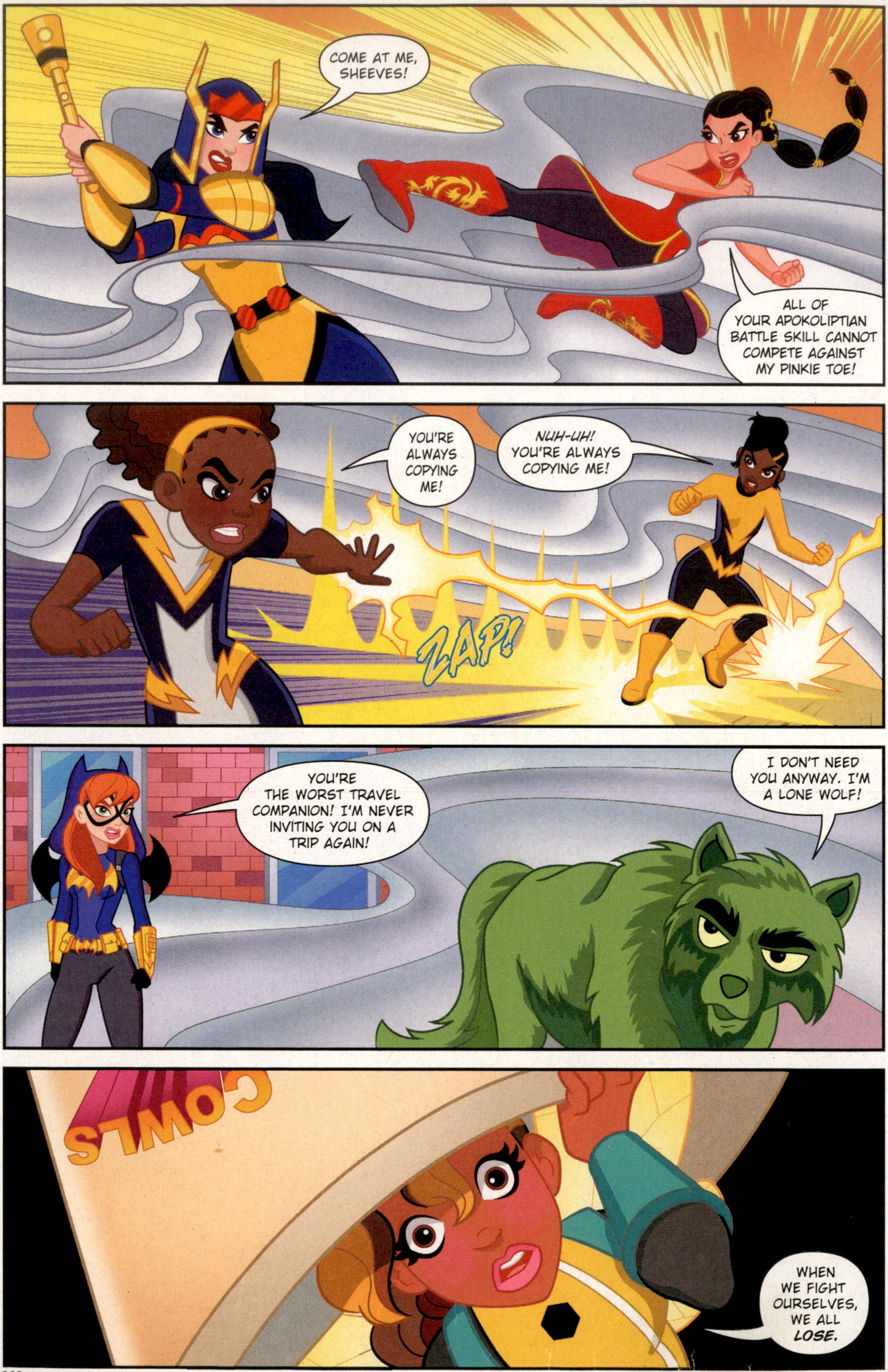

COME AT ME, SHEEVES!
ALL OF YOUR APOKOLIPTIAN BATTLE SKILL CANNOT COMPETE AGAINST MY PINKIE TOE!
YOU'RE ALWAYS COPYING ME!
NUH-UH! YOU'RE ALWAYS COPYING ME!
ZAP!
YOU'RE THE WORST TRAVEL COMPANION! I'M NEVER INVITING YOU ON A TRIP AGAIN!
I DON'T NEED YOU ANYWAY. I'M A LONE WOLF!
COWLS
WHEN WE FIGHT OURSELVES, WE ALL *LOSE.*

114

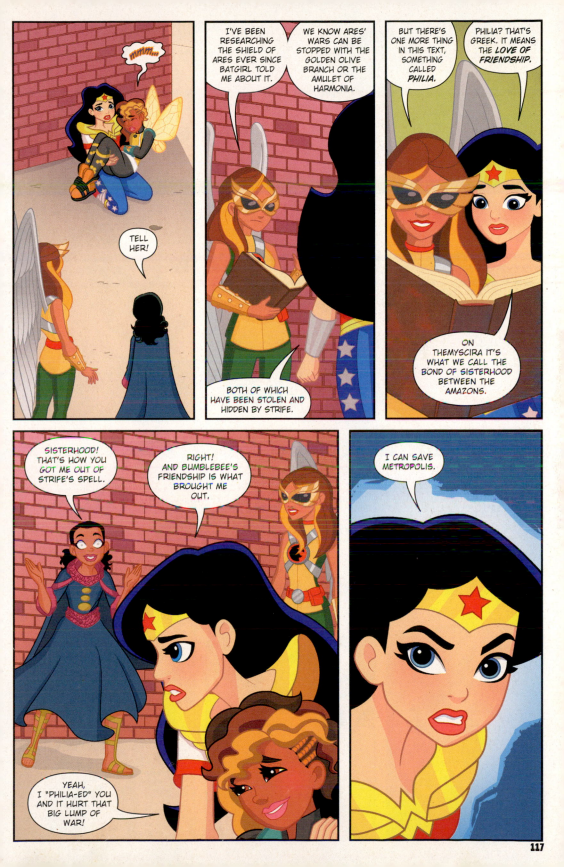

MMM...

TELL HER!

I'VE BEEN RESEARCHING THE SHIELD OF ARES EVER SINCE BATGIRL TOLD ME ABOUT IT.

WE KNOW ARES' WARS CAN BE STOPPED WITH THE GOLDEN OLIVE BRANCH OR THE AMULET OF HARMONIA.

BOTH OF WHICH HAVE BEEN STOLEN AND HIDDEN BY STRIFE.

BUT THERE'S ONE MORE THING IN THIS TEXT, SOMETHING CALLED PHILIA.

PHILIA? THAT'S GREEK. IT MEANS THE *LOVE OF FRIENDSHIP.*

ON THEMYSCIRA IT'S WHAT WE CALL THE BOND OF SISTERHOOD BETWEEN THE AMAZONS.

SISTERHOOD! THAT'S HOW YOU GOT ME OUT OF STRIFE'S SPELL.

RIGHT! AND BUMBLEBEE'S FRIENDSHIP IS WHAT BROUGHT ME OUT.

YEAH, I "PHILIA-ED" YOU AND IT HURT THAT BIG LUMP OF WAR!

I CAN SAVE METROPOLIS.

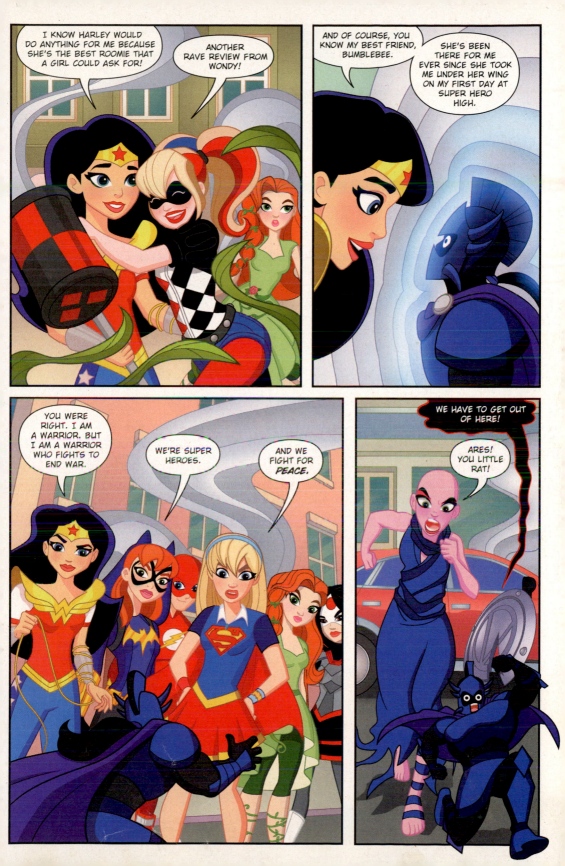

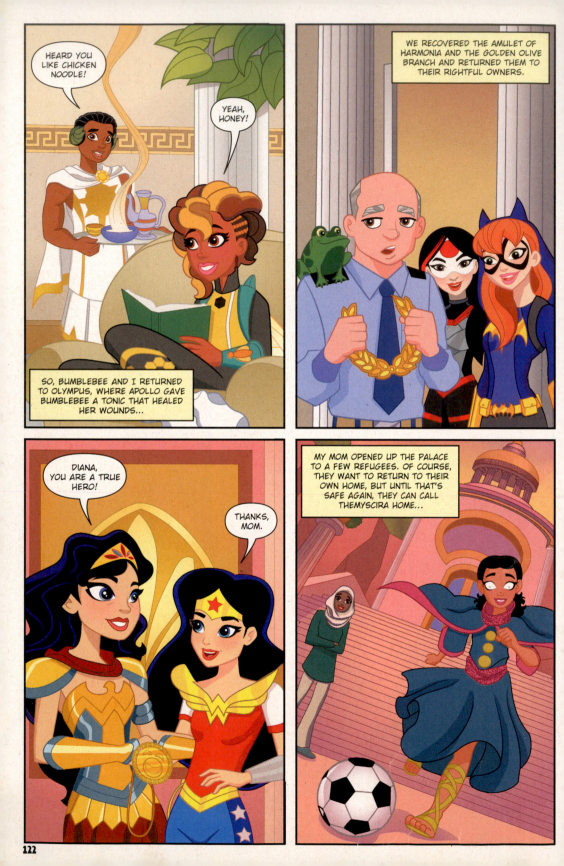

Panel 1:

HEARD YOU LIKE CHICKEN NOODLE!

YEAH, HONEY!

SO, BUMBLEBEE AND I RETURNED TO OLYMPUS, WHERE APOLLO GAVE BUMBLEBEE A TONIC THAT HEALED HER WOUNDS...

Panel 2:

WE RECOVERED THE AMULET OF HARMONIA AND THE GOLDEN OLIVE BRANCH AND RETURNED THEM TO THEIR RIGHTFUL OWNERS.

Panel 3:

DIANA, YOU ARE A TRUE HERO!

THANKS, MOM.

Panel 4:

MY MOM OPENED UP THE PALACE TO A FEW REFUGEES. OF COURSE, THEY WANT TO RETURN TO THEIR OWN HOME, BUT UNTIL THAT'S SAFE AGAIN, THEY CAN CALL THEMYSCIRA HOME...

I THANKED MY DAD FOR HIS OFFER TO MAKE ME A FULL GODDESS, BUT IT TURNS OUT, I LIKE ME JUST THE WAY I AM: HALF-GODDESS, HALF-AMAZON, A SUPER WEIRDO WHO'S ALL WONDER WOMAN.

I LIKE YOU JUST THE WAY YOU ARE, TOO, DIANA.

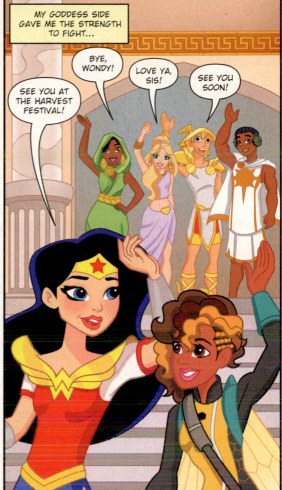

MY GODDESS SIDE GAVE ME THE STRENGTH TO FIGHT...

SEE YOU AT THE HARVEST FESTIVAL!

BYE, WONDY!

LOVE YA, SIS!

SEE YOU SOON!

MY AMAZON SIDE TAUGHT ME HOW TO LOVE MY FRIENDS AS SISTERS, AND THAT'S THE ONLY WAY WE BEAT ARES AND STRIFE...

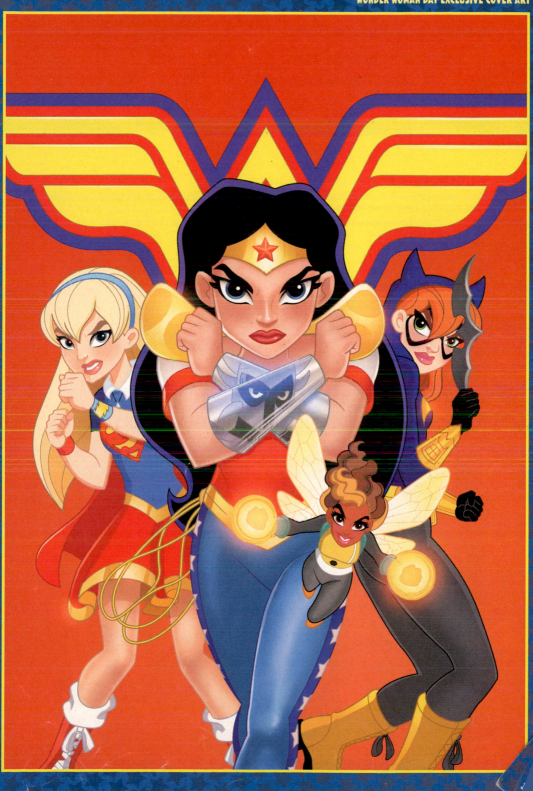

ABOUT THE AUTHOR

Shea Fontana is a writer for film, television, and graphic novels. In addition to the DC SUPER HERO GIRLS graphic novels, she also writes the *DC Super Hero Girls* animated shorts, TV specials, and movies. Her other credits include *Doc McStuffins, Disney's The 7D, Whisker Haven Tales with the Palace Pets,* live shows for *Disney on Ice,* and the feature film *Crowning Jules.* She lives in sunny Los Angeles, where she enjoys playing roller derby, hiking, hanging out with her dog, Moxie, and changing her hair color. ★

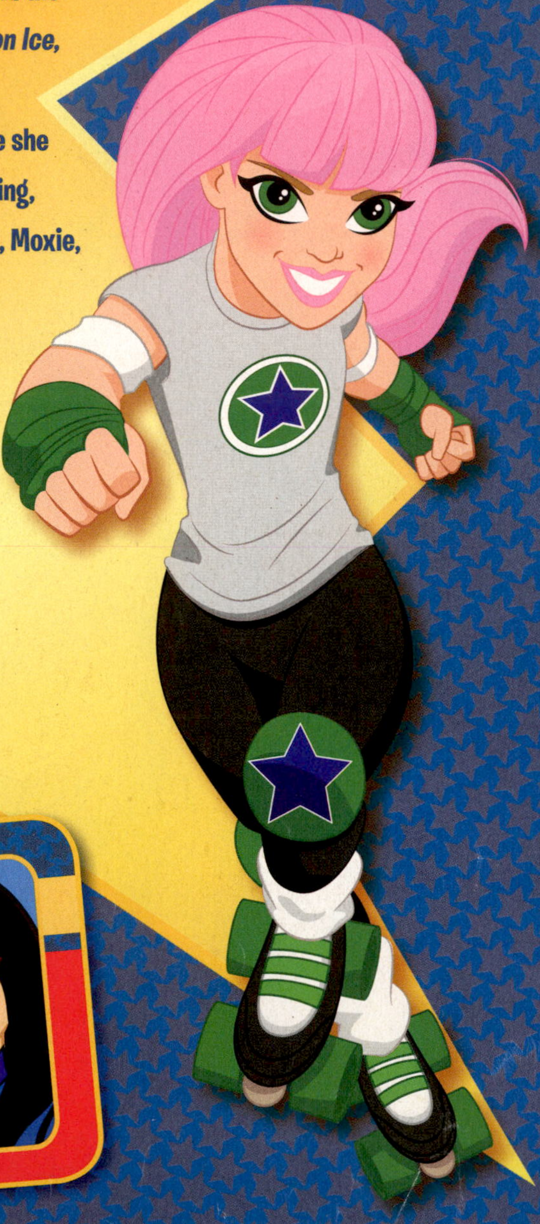

ABOUT THE COLORIST

Monica Kubina

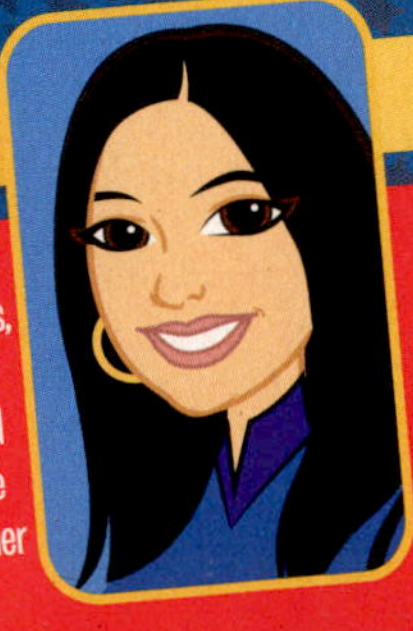

has colored countless comics, including super hero series, manga titles, kids' comics, and science fiction stories. She's colored *Phineas and Ferb, SpongeBob, THE 99,* and *Star Wars.* Monica's favorite activities are bike riding and going to museums with her husband and two young sons.

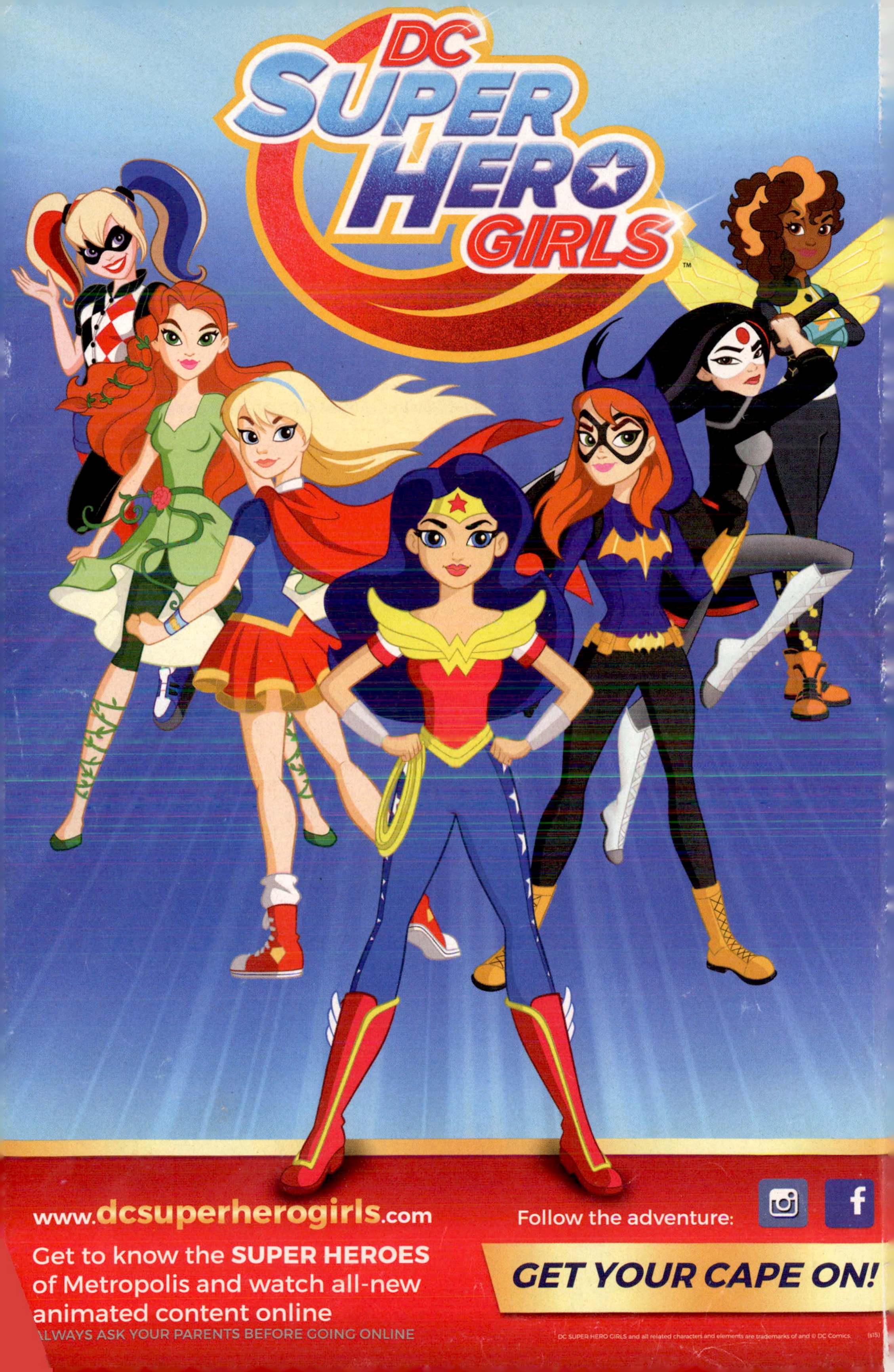
DC
SUPER HERO GIRLS
www.dcsuperherogirls.com
Get to know the SUPER HEROES of Metropolis and watch all-new animated content online
ALWAYS ASK YOUR PARENTS BEFORE GOING ONLINE
Follow the adventure:
GET YOUR CAPE ON!
DC SUPER HERO GIRLS and all related characters and elements are trademarks of and © DC Comics. (s15)

ABOUT THE ARTIST

Yancey Labat got his start at Marvel Comics before moving on to illustrate children's books, including *Hello Kitty* and *Peanuts* for Scholastic, as well as books for Chronicle Books, ABC Mouse, and others. His book *How Many Jellybeans?* with writer Andrea Menotti won the 2013 Cook Prize for best STEM (Science, Technology, Education, Math) picture book from Bank Street College of Education. He has two super hero girls of his own and lives in Cupertino, California. ★

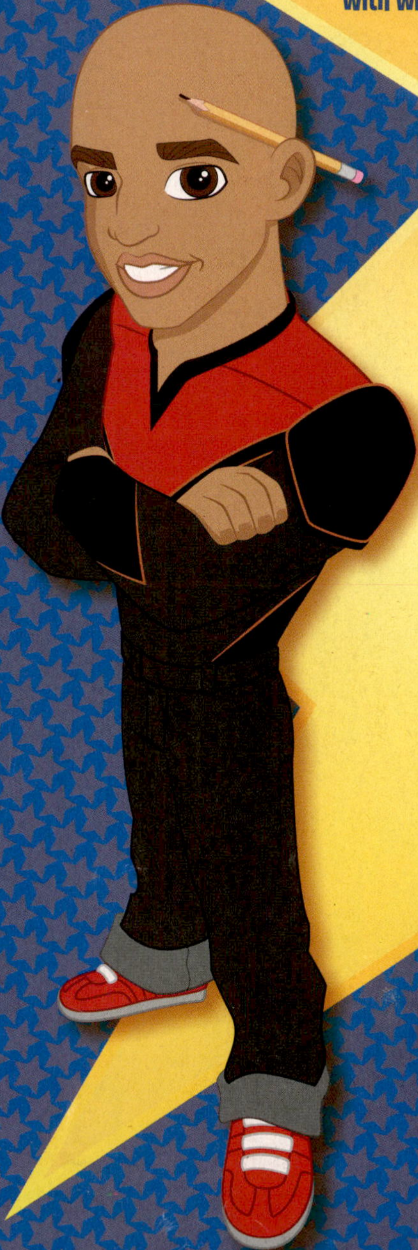

ABOUT THE LETTERER

Janice Chiang

has lettered *Archie, Barbie, Punisher* and many more. She was the first woman to win the Comic Buyer's Guide Fan Awards for Best Letterer (2011). She likes weight training, hiking, baking, gardening, and traveling.

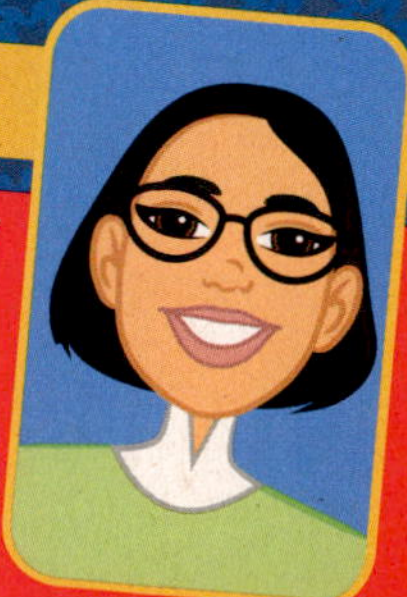